Discomania

Discomania by Jennifer Gibbons

Published in a hardback edition of 300 and an unlimited paperback edition.

All photographs of Jennifer Gibbons were taken when she was in Broadmoor Hospital, by an unknown photographer. The only dated photograph is the one of Jennifer on page *iv*, which was taken in 1982, when she was 19 years old.

Cover design by Ania Goszczyńska & Louise Mason
Cover lettering by Ania Goszczyńska
Text layout by Alena Zavarzina
Typeset in Caslon

ISBN: 9781913689919

Strange Attractor Press
BM SAP
London, WC1N 3XX, UK

Distributed by The MIT Press, Cambridge, Massachusetts.
And London, England.
Printed and bound in Estonia by Tallinna Raamatutrükikoda.

DISCOMANIA

JENNIFER GIBBONS

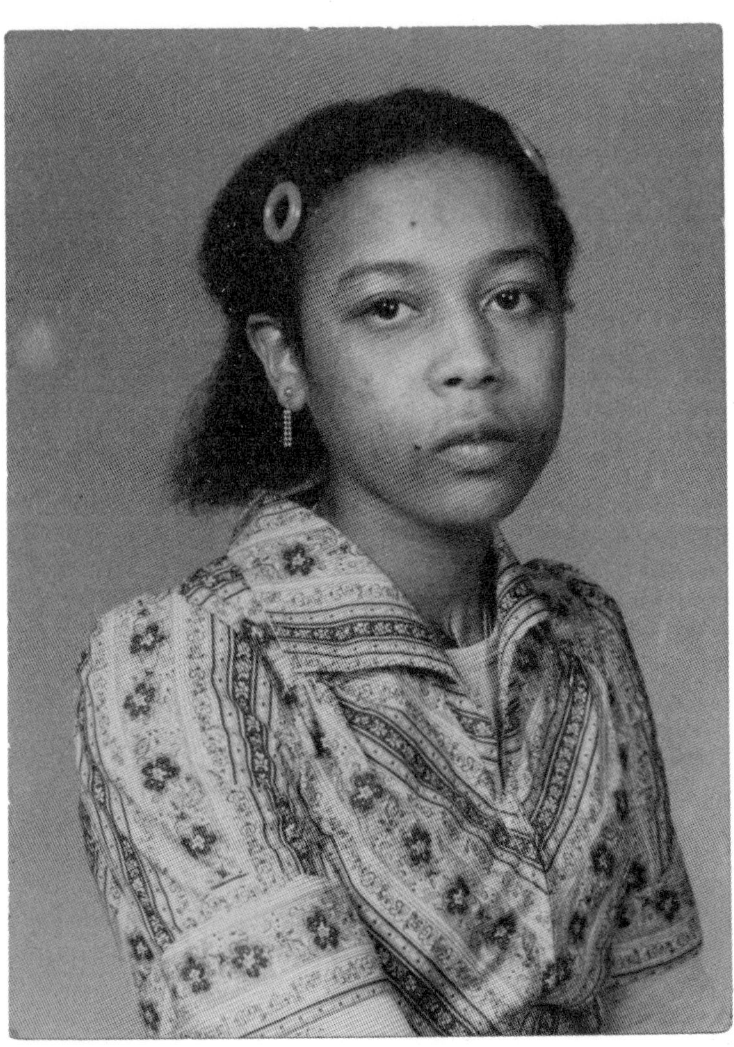

My lasting memory of Jennifer is,
how she pounded away
at her typewriter, well into
the early hours, writing a book
which she would name,
DISCOMANIA.
rejected at the time for
being too violent, sexual and
futuristic, Jennifer gave up
hope that one day her book
would be published;
from her her 16 year old
mind, comes the story of
dissatisfied teenagers,
roaming the streets of
America, searching for love.
this is her legacy –
DISCOMANIA.

June-Alison Gibbons
14 January 2025

EDITORIAL NOTE

Jennifer's style was as unique and unconventional as she was. Her spelling was her own, as was her punctuation. We have faithfully reproduced in this printed edition exactly how Jennifer wrote her book — June-Alison, Jennifer, and we, didn't wish to edit Jennifer's work into a conventional version of her text which didn't represent her.

We have silently corrected only those obvious misspellings which have resulted from Jennifer accidentally hitting the adjacent typewriter key to the one intended. In those few cases where we wondered whether a spelling accurately reflected Jennifer's idiosyncratic vision of that word, we have checked the typescript to see how she wrote it elsewhere. Sometimes Jennifer spells the same word in alternative ways throughout the novel, and indeed in her many other writings; again, we have striven to remain true to Jennifer's original text.

We discussed our editorial thoughts extensively, at the very start of this project, with June-Alison Gibbons, who also asked Jennifer — with whom June-Alison is in constant contact — for her opinions. Both Jennifer and June-Alison confirmed their absolute agreement with this, and our, approach.

Jennifer's typescript featured two possible endings, both of which are included in the present text. Each ending runs on from the final line of the main text, "Then truly I knew that none but one had managed to survive."

David Tibet and Ania Goszczyńska.
Hastings, St. Valentine's Day For Us All, 2025.

The road of life is rocky and you may stumble too..........

...........For the Gibbons's, the Hawkridge's and
the Miller's...........

This book is all about teen-ager's.......
specially created for today's and tomorrow's
teen-ager........... and has also been
written by a teen-ager.

I was fourteen when I was first introduced to the disco, by my cousin who is a very good dancer. I'm sixteen now and I still really love disco. I went to see saturday night fever with my schoolfriend's, Seth, Dalton, Season, Rocky and Veronica, and in time I learned all the step's. Infact I could do them almost as good as John Travolta.

I began to quit going to school, it got so bad that I even flunked most of the grade eight exam's, and I won several award's on the disco floor instead. Just dancing the day away.

Everywhere I went I would clear the dancing floor with my spectcular dancing, and it felt good to know that all the kid's were watching me in awe as I boogied to the Bus-Stop.

Then something happened. My father died in an auto wreck. I had been discoing at the club all night with my friend's, and it began to rain. My father was susposed to be coming to pick me up, but I did'nt realize it untill my mother rang me at Veronica's house the next morning and told me that he was killed instantly on the wet, slippery road, headed toward the disco club. After that the greiveing got so bad that I even began to blame myself for the accident. I felt guilty. That's when I started to write in my new red dairy. I brought it two week's after my father had died, and I have been writing down all sort's of minute thought's about my life eversince.

We moved house. My mother, my brother and I, soon after to a differnt street. Which was only accomplished after my plea was not to move to another town. It would have meant been seperated from my friend's and as we were to be a close bunch, I knew that it would only have made thing's all the worst. So we settled down in 2755 LeMond street, on the westside of the avenue, right near our high school and much nearer to my friend's home's. Veronica infact now only live's a couple of yard's away, but even then, after awhile I stopped going to the disco.

My reality began to get differnt from there. I no longer seemed to be in that state of anxiety to be on the disco floor. I alway's seemed to be either writing in my dairy or just re-reading it over and over again. And that's when Seth told me something that had me step back into reality again.

It had been after he had celebrated his fifthteenth birthday that we began to get romanticly involved. We all went to his party and had our self's a ball. Seth kept on gazing at me with his large, erotic, sensual brown eye's, and I incentively knew that he was commencing to get atracted to me. All night he walked around like a disco king, and all through his party he was summarly turned on.

He has a mound of shoulder length, thick darkbrown hair, and anybody including I can see lucidly that he is much better looking than either Dalton or Rocky. Maybe it's the fact that he had goodlooking parent's or maybe well I just guess he was born to be beautiful, and anyways most people are, and some of them are movie star's actually.

"How does it feel to be at my terrific, swell birthday party Livvy?" He asked me as I was drinking, by now my tenth glass of shandy and rum punch. Maybe my speech did sound a little slurred, but I did manage to say something.

"Dynamic."

"Terrific." He said.

"And how does it feel to be fifteen?" I asked.

He threw his arm's up into the hot air. "Beautiful sexy, something like you."

I did'nt even have enough time to jot that down in my beloved dairy because before I could say applejack's I and Seth were going out with each other.

We were going steady and it was a beautiful realationship. All the disirer's underneath the sun could'nt even describe what it was like, and up to now neither can I. But then maybe I oughta try.

It was blissful, it was strong, it was romantic, it was glamourosly sexual and it was Seth and it was me. We did everthing together that involved love. We went to the movie house, we roamed around town and when it was raining we went to the disco club. (Seth had finally dragged me with all his love back onto the dance floor) or we made love freguently in his old she-bang.

By the time we had lost our self's to each other, all the rest of the gang just had to simply beleive that Seth and I were ment for each other. It was a good thing to. Because then, sometime later we were all to find something out. Dalton was to be branded a homosexual. He told Season about himself one night as they perpared to get into bed, and then Season came to tell me about it.

"Dalton just told me, his eye's were aloof and sad and he looked like he was going to – cry."

"How.. many time's has he made love.. to you Season?" I asked, rememering how the first time I met him and how I alway's thought he was a little different from Rocky and Seth.

"It was going to be our fourth time we never got around to it, and so I just thought he was inlove with another girl, and that's when he told me."

"Maybe he's gay and hereosexual,.. or maybe he's just confused about
love." I said looking hopefully at Season's blank, pitiful blueyed face. "It's possible because he's only gone fourteen."

"It's not possible because he told me that he's erocticly inlove with Seth "

Season's voice had gone weak, and I had just been stung by a bee. "Dalton… is.. inlove – inlove with Seth?"

Season just gloomly nodded her head, and headed for the door, and I franticly ran my hand's through my hair and thought about Seth.

"He's – inlove with me?" Seth's expression was both surprized and equally flatterd.

We were all that's, Rocky, Veronica, Season, Seth and I, sitting inside his old she-bang, and Seth at the moment just was'nt loveing my story.

"I don'nt beleive it, ..hey is that true… Dalton hey y'all where's Dalton?" Seth was looking around wildly for this kid when he summarly walked in. Dalton wearing his usal blue-faded jean's and sleevless jean jacket just said "Hey everbody". And sat down beside us on the hay.

I looked across at Season, for a moment I thought she was going to fly the coop, but she just sat placidly where she was.

"Hey, Dalton are – you – really – inlove with – me?" Seth was stareing fixily at Dalton as though he'd never set eye's on him before. "Is it true that you find me sexually attractive?"

I wanted to laugh with hilarity, and so did Rocky and Veronica because they both had their hand's pressed tightly across their mouth's.

Dalton just was'nt going to say anything, so after awhile not to any bodie's surprized he picked himself up from the hay, his eye's were all sad and dark, that I thought he was going to... and headed toward the door's. Seth was stareing at the rooth, and for a moment I thought he was going to repair it.

Dalton's disaperance left each of the she-bang door's flapping fora while, it gave usall sometime to imagine his makeing love to a boy.

After the next few day's, Seth I knew was'nt about to take the whole thing as a serious story. He was emotionaly just to funny to be angry and so instead of doing his nut he laughed it of, and even pulled a few funny's about it all.

Beside's I reckon he was just getting excited about the disco on saturday. We all were infact and so was Dalton, even though he's no expert when it come's to doing the tango hustle.

Anyway's on saturday just before the disco I got mom to iron out my nearly-new-enough turquise dress. The one that I wore to Seth's 15th birthday party.

"Olivia, you are almost fifteen, I would have thought you could iron something by now." My mother said this while she was ironing my dress.

"I know, but I guess you really are a better ironer than me." I said while I combed a few tangle's out of my hair.

"She'll most probably hold up the iron the wrong way." My brother commented, he had just come back in from playing with his beloved moter bike and at the same moment I was wishing he could get back on it and fly the coop.

"Are you going to the disco tonight, or the movie house?"

"To the disco?" I replyed.

"Yeah because she's the disco queen of the 1980's, and she's got the fever man."

"Oscar calm up and go get a shower you look awful." My mother said truthfully. "And throw that bedraggled jean jacket of your's away".

"Don't worry now ladie's – I'm no skunk." He smiled wryly as he dispeared behind the door.

"What time are you going?" My mother had almost completed ironing my dress and my hair was still in tangle's.

"Oh around eight, Seth, Veronica and the other's are coming to callon me AND I guess I'll be back around midnight."

"And no later." Said my mother and I felt a little bit like cinderella, as she handed me my dress.

We were in the disco club and Seth, Dalton, Rocky, Veronica, Season and I danced madly for an hour.

The only thing I could see was Tee-shirt's, tight fitting pant's in shiny material, flimsy see through blouse's and a whole bunch of crazy dancing teen-ager's, getting sexually aroused as the stentorian ian sterophonic music filled through their system's.

It was hot and I saw Seth was pouring with sweat. I was too, and we entewined erocticly beneath the flashing light's.

"Come on y'all let's do the hustle, and shake our bootie's down to the ground." The d.J was screaming out over the music, and everbody was summarly dancing faster.

I found myself crazily in a differnt world as Seth grabbed hold of me swinging me around untill we were ingulfed totally by a bunch of scrimmageing, squirming snake's. Dalton beside us was hurling himself around at any boy and kissing them desirably untill they erocticly kissed him back.

They were all gay's and they were haveing the time of their live's. Touching, hugging and doing the freak. My ear's burned with music as well as the heat. "Let's sing Let's shout shake your body down to the ground ooh, shake your body down to the ground." Michale Jackson's voice rang out, and he had the power to send the room into shooting hysteric's, as teen-ager's everywhere threw up there arm's and shook there bodie's down to the ground.

I looked around and kid's had thrown themselve's onto the floor. They were sound's of sadism groaning as they tore at each other's clothe's half stripping themselve's so they could do everything they were susposed to be doing in bed.

The music changed tempo, and suddenly nobody was dancing. Instead their was hysterical mouth contact as drug pusher's of every kind fought to push pill's into frantic, desperate mouth's. They kissed amorously as the light's blacked out.

They came back on flashing crazily, as pill's and caspual's scatterd to the floor. Then there were kid's roaming the floor like a heap of desperate ant's as they fought preciously to get the pill's into their mouth's. Music filled my ear's, Seth was no where to be seen and Veronica and Rocky were still doing the hustle.

I twirled around, my feet still swaying to the beat. and saw Seth trying to break Dalton and another boy away from each other's. They were screaming at each other's and I knew they were haveing a fight. Seth was about to give up, when the boy summarely pushed him to the floor, he pushed Dalton aside and then they were like two fighting cock's again. It raced through my mind that he must have got jealouse when he saw Dalton kissing with another boy. After all they were gay.

Seth picked himself up from the floor. The music seamed louder and I herd myself, through the music calling his name. He waved to me, then we found ourselve's back together, scuttleling through the crowd and heading for the entrance of the disco.

We sat sublunary on the sidewalk for a moment as we got our breath's back, it was dark and the star's were shining stupendously.

Then Seth looked at me, his brown eye's were huge with disbeleive. "Hey, Olivia – your right – cause our freind Dalton is really gay heck I don't beleive it – he was in there actually trying to tear the pant's of this other guy and then when he could'nt get them of he turned on him like a scurrilous monkey and lashed him in the eye's."

I nodded my head, my mind reaming back into the disco inferno. "I guess he just love's boy's better than he love's girl's."

"Yeah – but whatta bout me – where do I stand when he start's trying to tear the pant's of me – and Rocky?"

"On your own two feet, beside's you and Rocky are much stronger than him." I shrugged my shoulder's and began to enjoy the cool evening air.

"Aw hell, that ain't fair I'm gonna have to kick him out the gang, I mean how can I stick it when Dalton's gonna be stareing at me all over, like I'm some eroctic sex symbol."

I looked up at the moon for a while. Then I looked back at Seth's slightly growing, angry face. He had finally woken up. "Seth, what does it matter." I explained. "I'm a girl, and I'm in love with you and as long as you don't make any surreptitious advance's to him, everthing's going to be okay – and beside's it won't be fair eiether if you push him out the gang."

"And why not?" Seth asked propping up his knee's, and summarly putting his forehead on them.

"Because, he's our freind Seth, and after all he's only human."

I managed to reason with him in the end, and it meant that Dalton could stay in with the gang. Beside's Dalton I found really is a nice curly headed, brown haired kid, and what does it matter I thought as I opened up my dairy, if he is a gay.

It did'nt really matter to us, but it did matter to Season because a few day's after she found out that her boyfriend was a definate homosexual she tried unsuccessfully to commit suicide.

It was while we were in school, Seth, Rocky, Veronica, Dalton and I that Season went of her nut and summarly threw herself through her bedroom window.

I had'nt wonderd why she was'nt in school that day, neither had the other's. Because we all decided it was the disco. After all it did go on untill two in the morning. Then we all went to call on her after school and that's when we found out. Her mother opened the door and we could all tell that she had been crying.

"Hi can we talk with Season awhile?" I asked trying not to sound too happy.

"Season is'nt feeling to well. She's just tried to commit suicide." Her voice was slow and weak and I felt mine was going to do the same.

"Commited suicide." Said Dalton. "Hey that's dumb."

Rocky elbowed him in the rib's and told him to be quiet, or he would be trying to do the same too.

"Has she been hurt bad?" Asked Seth.

"No, but she could have been killed, and she still has'nt told me or her father why she did it."

Seth looked at me, I looked at Veronica and she looked at Dalton. We could all see that he was beginning to feel slightly sub conoisous, and I was thinking he would say something about Season but he did'nt he just backed away, and started to amble away down the sidewalk.

"Hey Dalton, come back here – I thought you told us you wanned to see sombody." Rocky yelled.

Dalton did'nt say anything, do anything, but he just walked on and that as far as we could see was that.

When we all turned back round, Season was standing in the doorway clad in her night-gown and a bandage wrapped around her wrist.

"Hi freind's, how was school today?" She asked in a more than cheerful voice. "I guess you had a horrific day."

I looked into her eye's, and I could see that she was still sad. "The usall." Said Veronica "And we all missed you like hell."

She smiled and we saw as her eye's slightly wonderd over to Dalton's form as he ambled down the street.

"Did you enjoy the disco last night?" She asked.

"It was swell... and it was hot stuff." Said Rocky "And man was I dancing."

"Will you be in school tomorow?" I asked. Speaking for the first time.

"Yeah, and I'll be at the disco tonight as well, mom say's I can go any time I like."

Neither of us decided to say anything about her banaged wrist, because it was lucid that she had forgoton all about it.

"We'll see you tonight." Said Seth. "Meet us outside the drugstore okay, and then we can walk from there to the disco club."

Season nodded her head. "Okay I'll be there."

It was hot, the disco floor was crowded and I summarly turned to put a dime in the vending machine. Seth was somewhere in the crowd dancing energeticly like a peacock, and I wondered if he would ever get tired. I drank my soda pop. The music and the flashing red and blue light's were all inspired dramaticly as the beat of the rolling drum's yelled out.

Kid's everywhere were just dancing normally and some where kissing or hugging each other. I did see Dalton once, and he was busy getting sexually aroused by a tall, long blondehaired boy.

I finnished my soda pop and then found myself back on the dancing floor. Somewhere behind me Veronica and Rocky were haveing the time of their young live's. So was I but I could'nt find Seth to share it with, so I just danced by myself for a while.

My eye's wannerd over to where Season and a colored guy were dancing themselve's dizzy. They were swinging wildly to the music, and I saw that Season was laughing with joy.

I smiled at her and she looked at me with huge, dazzling dilated eye's then waved at me summarly before the colored boy smothred her with kiss's, and hustled her out of sight.

The music was deafening, and Seth came back to me as I started to sing to some of the word's. "Your the one that I want...you are the one I want ooh.. ohh your the one that I want"

Seth pulled me into his arm's and we danced like mad for a moment.

Then the music changed, and we watched as everybody went mad like hysterical. There were teen-ager's all around jumping on top of each other. Pulling anybody to the floor and salaciously going frenzie. They screamed loudly to the music, pulling out blade's and stabbing their best freind's to death.

A boy came staggering toward us with blood dripping from his tee-shirt and his hands pressed tightly over his stomach. I watched horrifeid as he collasped to the ground with convulsion's worst than an epilepsy fit. The whole place was a phenomenon, and Seth was yelling to me over the drumb pounding music to get out. He grabbed hold of my hand and we stumbled over a floor of hysterical kid's full of concupiscence and stabbing knife's.

Police siren's and shreiking, pericing amberlance bell's filled my ear's as Seth and I reached the entrance. Blindly the only thing I could think of was Veronica, Rocky, Dalton and Season. Where were they? Were they alright? Did they escape from it alive like we did?

"Seth wait." I yelled. "what about the other's did you see them come out with us?"

Seth said something, but I could'nt hear because of the piricing police siren's now filling my ear's like something out of the Burmuda triangle. We mounted the sidewalk and collapsed onto it as an amberlance came screeching around the corner. My eye's were filled with a million red star's, and then I saw Dalton, Veronica and Rocky came running from the entrance of the building.

"Quick where's Season?" Yelled Rocky. "We have to get outta here, cause the fuzz is around."

"Where the hell is she?" Yelled Seth. "I thought she came out with us."

We all ran half way back toward the building, but then stopped aruptly as two cop's came flying toward us. We changed direction and scatterd amongest the commotion of parked abulance's and police car's.

I lost hold of Seth's jacket and found myself running around on my own. I was like a crazy yo-yo for a moment until the cop's gave up chaseing and summarly turned to chase some more kid's.

When I stopped spinning I looked around franticly for Seth and the other's but they had all gone like the wind and disapeared into thin air.

Hastily for some reason I found myself running back toward the bellowing building. I could only see Season in my eye's and I knew suddenly that I just had to find her. I doged a herd of stampeading kid's and headed for a pile of caualtie's laying outside the entrance. Season was no where to be seen, I was heading to go back inside when I saw her been carried away on a strecther. Was I haveing illusion's? I ran up beside it, franticly calling out her name. Her long blonde hair was tragedly disarayed and satuated with blood as it lay over her sickly contused face.

"Season". I yelled. "Can you hear me?" I knew that she was unconious because her eye's were closed. But I still wanted her to open them and say something. Then I saw as one of the ambulance men pulled the comforter right over her face. He looked at me and shook his head.

"Sorry kid, she's dead."

"Dead." I screamed. "She can't be it's impossible she can't be dead."

The ambulance man just contiued to shake his head. then he disapeard into the darkness.

I watched horrifeid as Season was higherd up in to the ambulance. My heart was pounding with something like ice. I tried to grab at the comforter. To pull it away from her inocent face. "Season." I screamed "Sea-son."

But they closed the ambulance door's and I was lost in the crowd of stampeading teen-ager's.

I stumbled home, and the moon was shining bright, and the sky was dark like ebony, and the tear's were in my eye's because my best freind Season had just died from the power's of a tragic discomania, in which only more were to follow.

It was almost midnight when I opened my dairy and wrote in it.

July 21st 1983
Season tried to kill herself today. She can't stand Dalton been a gay. I knew that she was sad, when we went to call on her after school. We went to the disco, the scene was scurrilous, lot's of people died and one of them was "Season". Her life was a happy one, but she died inocent and young.......

After Season's death I don't think any of us really got back to our usall self's. Dalton was the one who I knew was hurt the most. It was vizuble all over his face. His eye's would fill with tear's at the slightest mention of her name.

We did'nt go to her funeral because we all knew we would die from greive if we did, and none of us wanted to go and face her mother again. It would have been too lamented.

For about two week's we all played hooky. We just sat in Seth's old she-bang either crying out our heart's or dreaming of Season, when she was with us and when she was alive with love for the apple of her eye's, Dalton.

He disappeared about a week later, Seth and I had said nothing to hurt his feeling's, and neither had Veronica or Rocky. But I guess we knew we had it comming sooner or later, because he was'nt speaking to neither of us those two week's after Season's funeral.

When Seth spoke to him he would just pretend he was'nt there, and gaze through the air as though he was seeing an illusion before wiping away the tear's from his eye's.

We stopped going to the disco for awhile. Then we found that Rocky was begging to find drug's as some more close time soulmate's. He was smokeing marijuana, and he told us that his parent's were threatning to throw him out the house unless he quit smoking it. He come's from a large family with six brother's and sister's and we all knew that was enough without one of them becomming a drug adict, but his love for his new discovery was too great and so he prlonged to use it and ened up makeing us use it too. Marijuana is'nt too bad a drug so I guess Rocky did us all a favor in introducing it like he did. It was a beautifull experince. It made me feel wonderfully lightheaded and dreamy.

When I was'nt sober I was either gazing at large floating color's or listening to music. My day's were longer. Five minute's seemed like one hour and one week seemed like half a year.

We were all laying sleeply in the she-bang one noon, when Dalton summarly came in from no where paticular. He was wearing this huge stetson hat, and the wide smile on his face was more than we could prove to been just happy. He waved to us and slumped down on the hay beside Veronica and Rocky. "Hi kid's." He said. "Y'all sure did miss me like hell did'nt you?"

"Yeah, and where the god darn hell have you been?" Slurred Seth. "We been.. ripping our brain's out looking for you."

I could tell that Dalton knew that something had happened to us. He kept sniffing around the air and stareing at us with a bewilderd aspect.

"Hey guy's don't you know where I been – I've been around the state's four time's and back."

We all laughed like mad for a while, and Dalton was laughing his head off too. We could'nt beleive that he was actually one of us again. "And you know kid's – guess what kid's I'm not ever gonna take that trip again, because as sure as hell did I miss you."

"Yeah and we missed you too." Said Rocky handing him one of our marijuana ciggerate's. "Smoke this and your gonna be in paridise." We all watched as Dalton now even more bewiderd took the joint between his finger's, shrugging his shoulder's as Rocky lit it up for him. "Hey, now what is this?" He asked, speaking to nobody in paticular.

"It's great, and your gonna feel it." Laughed Seth. "Your gonna be floating of the ground like you ne-ver floated before."

Veronica, Rocky, Seth and I were all waiting dreamly for him to take a few drag's of the ciggerate, but he never. Instead he just threw it down into the hay and got up and headed for the door. Neither of us could have the strength to call him back, so we just lay there.

A moment later he came back a huge back pack slung across his shoulder and a big mysterious grin on this face. "Okey kid's sit up this is my duty, I have some great return pressent's for you all." Seth and I sat up, he leaned on me weakly and I slumped back into the hay again. We all watched sleeply as Dalton swiftly undid the back bag and brought out a cluster full of wrapped item's.

"Aw gee, you are kind." Veronica yawned. "Have you brought us all some thing as nice as candy?"

Rocky was still busy with the marijuana ciggerate, trying his best to light it up again when Dalton summarly plunked him on his dark head and handed him one of the colorfull package's. "Here you go buddy, this is for you." Rocky turned around surprized, and took the package. We all watid eageraly for him to unwrappe it. He laughed loudly as the paper began to slip away, and then we all found out what he was laughing about. It was because of the fact that Dalton had just brought him a brand new action man doll, and to make matter's seem even crazier, the doll looked just like him. "Hey, Dalton this is even better than what I had for christmas seven year's ago." Rocky was laughing like a hysterical hyenia, and we all thought he would never be able to stop.

"Okay now kid's unwrapp the rest of my dutie's." Said Dalton somemore colorful package's into Veronica's, Seth's and my hand's.

"Hey this is beautiful." Laughed Veronica hugging tightly a little yellow teddy bear to her chest. "Dalton I love it."

"Oh, Dalton this is wonderful." I half laughed and yawned as I pulled away the paper and held in my hand's a beautiful blonde haired barbie doll. "Dalton, it's beautiful." I stopped yawning summarly and gazed down more intensely as it lay in it's little light blue dress and red push on shoe's. She looked just like Season, her face was so inocent and young, with her beautiful, dazzling blue eye's and her small, cute baby like nose.

Dalton was smiling at me and I ran my finger's slowly thrue her long blonde, shining hair....

"Hey, Dalton whered you get this from, this is terrific." Seth was laughing, as he flaunted a gleaming silver chain admiringly around his neck. "Hey did you buy it down Manhattan Dalton... you've even managed to get my name fixed on it?"

Dalton nodded his head and came to help Seth as he put it on. I smiled and watched with surprize as Seth suddenly whirled around and took Dalton into his arm's smothering him with kiss's and hug's. "Thank's Dalty boy, I swear I'll keep it for as long as I shall live."

Dalton stood back and laughed slightly, shrugging his shoulder's as he looked enchantingly around the she-bang.

I knew that he had just been sexually aroused, by Seth's reaction and at that moment I was feeling pretty glad that he was'nt a girl.

In a while we were all laying back down dreamily in the hay, smokeing our marijuana, and basicly just hitting the sack. Rocky for sometime had still been trying Dalton out to take a drag of his ciggerate. But when he collsped on the hay and would'nt, Rocky put his arm around him and laughed and they both ended up hitting the sack together.

I went home that night to write in my dairy, and the little doll that Dalton had given me, came with me.

August 11th 1983

Dalton came back today.

We were laying in the she-bang smokeing Rocky's marijuana, and he came in looking happier than I've ever seen him since Season's death. He brought us present's. Mine was a doll. She look's just like Season and I know that Dalton brought it for a reason.......

We all started to go back to the disco club after that. I think it was the fact that Dalton (Dalty boy) had come over Season's death so well. We would all have hallucination's, makeing ourself's go wild with fright that one day he would end up commiting suicied or just summarly disapear again. But he did'nt because I guess he knew that we would miss him awfully if he did.

When I told my mother and Oscar about Season's death, they just acted as though they did'nt want to know about it. I knew then that it was because she had been trampled to death in the disco instead of having died naturally from an illness or something. But I did want them to feel sorry for her. Even if at the time I was going to the same kind of disco club when the tragedy happened.

I named my little barbie doll after her, because I think Season is a beautiful name, and I kept her sitting beside the mirror on my dresser for sometime so that she could share with me all the little secret's that I wrote down in my dairy. Season was somebody that I would never forget, because my heart was alway's beside her no matter what I did or where I went.

We went to the disco on monday night, Seth, Veronica, Rocky, Dalty boy and I, and we were all on the dance floor for about three hour's non stop. It was decided on behalf of Season that we should'nt smoke anymore of Rocky's marijuana. We all wanted to be wide awake incase of another disco mania.

It was hot, music engulfed, and jam packed with jamming teen-ager's. Somewhere on the dance floor Seth was dancing with me like another John Travolta and I was dancing with him like another Olivia Newton-John. We did the sidewalk bump, the disco duck and the Lindy hustle.

We rubbed shoulder's with any body not careing either if we did have our toe's stamped a couple of ocassion's.

"Ain't no stopping us now." Blared above our head's sending vibration's of rhythmical scream's through our system's.

My eye's were summarly overcome by a galaxy of misty multicolored clothe's as kid's sqirmed imperiously to the vigorous music. My feet stepped simultaneously in time to the beat of drum's. Seth smiled rouseingly makeing me feel absorbed with new exhilaration, his eye's penetrated me erocticly feverousily with excitement, as my hair brushed tremorously against his bare arm's. The music made us dance faster as it summarly changed tempo, and Seth put his arm's around my waist with the flying swiftness of an octopus.

Then somebody screamed hysterically into the music and everbody went crazy. They jumped up to the flashing light's trying frenziely to pull them apart. Knifeing each other with sharp pointed blade's untill they were satisfeid with the spurting, unstaunching blood of best buddie's and stranger's. I watched astoundingly as one boy ripped of his shirt and pulled it tightly around the neck of another, he was screaming emboldenly as his body jerked hysterically to the stenorian music. My heart lurched as Seth summarly flew from my side He disapeared behind a stampeading gang of scurrilous centipead's and screaming blade clucthing bull's.

I tried desperately to move my feet, they were souround by a heap of blood coverd clawing hand's. My mind was swaying mistly toward's the entrance of a huge mulitícolore picture. I saw as two girl's tried deleriously to tear each other's clothe's off with flashing blade's. My eye's wanderd summarly to a bunch of screaming wild girl's as they savagely pounced onto a boy, pushing him to the floor, swiping his face with there tightly clenced fist's, as they stimulously done him over.

The place was full of swarming, pugnacious, dangerous miscellneous reptile's. Two boy's stamped the brain's out of another one while he lay screaming helplessy on the floor. Teen-ager's everywhere pounded their way ontop of each other crazily strangling, biteing and slashing each other's with broken glass, smashed record's or sharpened blade's.

I gaped dizzly horrified. A girl ran screaming into my direction bannishing a sharp edged blade, she waved it in front of me threateningly as she motioned it in time to the drum's of music. Then she summary swung around and slashed violently at a boy's face. He viscously pushed her to the floor, before salaciously pepareing to fornicate with her.

I managed to move my feet, before franticly screaming out for Seth.

Somebody from behind me summarly swung their arm's around my neck. It was as though the whole building had gone pitch black. Then I suddenly saw some thing filled with color's spin away from eye's. The shreiking sound of a police siren acompanied by the sudden, high pitched scream of a girl swarmed throughout the buliding as I saw Seth's bloodied form come hurling back to me. He lashed out for the arm's around my neck prizing them apart, and finally he kicked down the slashed faced boy to the floor.

I found myself suddenly falling as Seth grabbed hold of my hand hastly and pulled me through the motionless crowd. We ran on, then somebody shouted. "It's the fuzz." And everbody went crazy again. Team's of cop's charged in all holding raised gun's and waveing them toward any kid. "Okay everbody stay right where you are, don't nobody move." Yelled a cop. "We aim to kill if any of you move."

A boy ran hysterically toward him waveing a blade. The cop swung around and shot him in the stomach. Everbody began to yell. They lunged forward takeing it in turn's to wrestle with a cop. A loud clamor of bullet's rang out and I could no longer hear the music. Two boy's grabbed hold of a cop before he could manage to fire his gun. They kicked him to the floor, then fell heavly on top of him as two bullet's whistled through the air cutting sharply through their head's.

Seth and I tried to reach the entrance, but two cop's stood bannishing gun's. "Okay every single, one of you cunt's hold up." A cop yelled as he ran into the crowd and wrestled with a screaming girl. The girl kicked out and four savageing boy's stabbed the cop frenziely over again.

Seth pulled me nearer to the entrance, and I found myself biteing into my lip with fright. "Get your ass's back." Yelled the cop aiming this gun straight at Seth. "Each and every godamed one of you are under arest."

Seth said something, and I yelled frantcily to him as he tried to wrestle with the cop. The cop suddenly forgot to fire his gun. he brought it down hard across Seth's face and pushed us back into the crowd. "Now get back there you bastard's and raise your hand's into the air." Seth was yelling something to the cop as we picked ourself's up. We did'nt see or hear as he was savagely stabbed to the floor by six hysterical youth's. But we only looked up and saw how empty the way to the entrance was. We ran toward it without seeing another cop. But as we ran across the street I could hear the sound of following feet.

I turned my head still ran and caught sight of three shaddow's running after us, then one of them yelled my name and I knew who they were.

"Seth." I yelled. "Waite it's Veronica and Rocky and Dalton."

We stopped running and stood breathlessly on the sidewalk waiteing for them to catch us up. Under the moonlight I glanced at Seth and regonized horrificly the large purple, swollen bump ontop of his eye. Seth seemed to be totally unware of it as he waited for the rest to hurry up, but under the moonlight it looked so crusome and big that I thought he must be blind.

"Seth you look beautiful." Rocky yelled. "Hey whered you get that thing?"

"What thing?"

"That thing – the one that's makeing you look like a batterd pizza." Rocky pointed to his eye, and Seth summarly touched it and winched. "Ow – that hurt's – fuck that bastard of a cop."

We all laughed and then Rocky showed us his gashed arm. His eye's turned now as he held it out. "See that – some crazy girl did that, stabbed me with a blade – and man did I want to whup her one."

"And why did'nt you?" Seth asked.

"I'm in need of something hot – hey Dalty boy you wanna help me wreck a store?"

Dalty boy shook his head. "No thank's, anyway's what kind of store?"

"The drug's store man."

"My mom's gonna kill me." Seth was dabbing at his closed eye with his jacket sleeve.

"Don't you think you already dead?" I asked. "I mean you look as though you've just stepped out from a volcano."

"I'm going home now okay?" Veronica said.

I swung around to face her, and thought imeditately that she rather resembled a scarecrow. Her titian colored hair was all over the place, some of it even standing up on end's.

"But ain't you gonna help us raid the store?" Yelled Rocky. "Baby I can't be with out you."

I linked my arm's with her, looking at her sleepy expression. "I guess you want to get your beauty sleep huh?"

"I'm just tired Livvy and I need some rest." She smiled at me and then she departed across the street. "See you around sometime okay."

"See you around Veronica."

"Yeah see you around sometime Veronica AND I promise I'll bring back some of that high stuff for you." Rocky waved to her and swaggerd down the street.

"Hey are'nt you gonna take her home?" Said Seth watching her amble down the street.

"Hey has'nt she got leg's." Veronica turned back to wave to wave at him. "And beside's the feeling to do it is in me now."

We all waited outside the drugstore. Then Rocky who had somehow persuaded Daltyboy to help him smashed the brick through the reflection plauged window and yelled "Man I love the sound of breaking glass." Seth and I stood back as he and Daltyboy smashed their way through and disapeared inside. I was shivering slightly as the sound of spattering pill's and bottle's filled my ear's. This whole episode to me was like one big midnight dream, and Seth was just doing notthing except wiping his jacket sleeve peepettually across his damaged eye.

The moon above us in the black starlit sky was slowly beginning to fade away and I wonderd vaguely weather we would be here all night. There was the biggest explosion from inside the store, and that's when the alarm bell went off.

We saw as Rocky and Daltyboy came stumbling out ladend with package's and bottle's, their eye's suddenly wide awake with surprize then Seth and I saw no more as we both flew the coop.

Police siren's filled my ear's, I pulled Seth hastily into a side way ally as both of us had already out run the other's. There was this loud dramatic sreech of tyer's. Rocky was scuttling in one direction and Daltyboy was scuttling to another, untill he tripped over a pile of bottle's and fell sprawlingly to the ground. He picked himself up and tried to run, but ened up limping instead.

Then that's when the car's sreeched to a halt, almost beneath him and sent him running like an athlecic into Rocky's direction. There was this other screaming, terrific sound and I watched hopelesly as Rocky shot back up the street been chased like a hound by a police car. It was smart of the cop's and so Rocky and Daltyboy were finally caught and pushed into the back of the police car. Handcuffed and requistely angry.

It's weird that Seth and I were never caught, but then we were both hideing in the ally way, and beside's we we'rnt the one's who broke into that drugstore. It was Rocky and Daltyboy to be frankfully honest, and Seth was still tending to his eye when it all happened.

I wrote everything down in my dairy that night, with Season there to read it with me. She seemed surprized as she did.

August 13th 1983
There are red's green's and blue's in my life, "D" and "R" have been caught by the blue siren's. (Raiding a drugstore). The disco is red, as with murder and blood. My life is still free from it as with the green's of the grass and the tree's.

I should never have gone to school the next day because there was a dramatic scene in which five kid's were killed and the math teacher Mr. Odessy. He was strung up like a chicken, and was struggling so badly that I think he deid of a heart attack. He had a purple face, his toungh was hanging and his eye's popped out like tennis ball's.

Kid's screamed out "We want disco we want disco we want disco." Tearing up their school book's, smashing up shelve's and table's they tore the place apart, attacking any teacher who got in the way. I for one moment relized that I was back in the disco.

It all started when one of the eighth grader's, Ojay Wargacki went berserk after mr Odessy told him to quit playing his transistor radio. Ojay suddenly stood up and started wrecking the place to peice's while he screamed of his head to the world. "We want music to hell with this lousy godamed crap" and "your not gonna make us do any of it either you hear?"

I saw as Mr. Odessy went bright red. "Sit down Wargacki and get on with your work, your not the boss of this class I am."

Ojay went hysterical and threw the transistor at him. "Go to hell your word's don't mean a thing." Then he grabbed his book's and started tearing them to shread's.

"Wargacki." Mr. Odessy was really shouting his word's out now. "Don't you use that language in this school – get back to your work and shut up, you'll earn notthing from this."

Wargacki threw a table at him and suddenly went quite for a moment as he slowly looked around at us, a smile on his face before pulling out something small and glinting from his boot. It was a blade and I felt my heart lurch.

"I don't need punk's to tell me what to do with life, lousy math teacher, I only need my parent's to tell me and their dead." Jay flicked open the pen-knife and smashed a chair flying as he went for Mr Odessy.

Mr Odessy dodge him behind the table, suddenly going calm. "Now listen to me Wargacki, put away that knife and sit down please."

"No." Screamed Ojay. "Your notthing but a lousy backward punk and if I'm gonna earn anything it's gonna be you."

Somebody screamed in the back row as Wargacki like a let losed, wild animal suddenly lunged himself on Mr Odessy, the table came flying across the room, missing me by inch's as it smashed it's way through a window.

Mr Odessy was screaming like something I've never heard in my life. So were kid's as they struggled over to him, kicking, shakeing and plunking with ruler's and chair's. I saw as they hauled him up by his collar's and threw him up against a cupboard as Ojay ramshacked it, pulling out a peice of robe and strung him up like a run away chicken. I was been hurled to the front by hysterical kid's, when Mrs Sansorton suddenly opened the door and walked in.

She was imediately grabbed by the mob and dragged over to where Mr Odessy was haveing something like a heart attack. Then she cried out. "All of you get back into your seat's, all of you – this moment – all of you please get back."

Ojay slapped her repeatly around the face and was yelling something that was too loud for me to hear as the kid's charaged to the front. Then I saw as Jolene Summor's, Delila Cazzat, Wilma Cassidy and Jody Schatzberg all started to forcefully tear of her clothe's. They were pulling down her chicon hair do and letting her hair roam free.

"Children – stop it – stop it – at – once." Mrs Sansorton's voice was no longer loud but had suddenly modifyed instead. As she tried to break free I was yelling out to her "Mrs Sansorton, Mrs Sansorton get away and try and get to the door." She was my fravoit teacher and now she was been molested by her own pupil's.

Ojay was pulling her to the ground, while the other's got set to string her up. Just like Mr. Odessy who I now guessed must be dead. Seth and I ran to the door's his eye was still bad and he was going to stay home today, but I was suddenly glad that he did come in.

Ojay yelled. "C'mon now let's go get the rest." Everbody stopped what they were doing and ran hysterically after us out through the door's. They were yelling out. "We want disco we want disco."

"Yeah let's make that clear." Yelled Ojay. "We want disco and these lousy creep's are gonna give it to us."

At least five kid's must have been trampled in the stampead. As Ojay lead the way to the teacher's center. He was yelling all the time and so were the other's. Veronica, Seth and I decided not to follow them, but instead we went back to the class room and found that Mrs Sansorton was already free and trying to unbound Mr. Odessy. I could already see that he was dead and so could Veronica and Seth. We ran over to him and helped Mrs Sansorton with the rope.

"I'm alright." She said. "But I don't think Mr. Odessy is, those stupid wreckless kid's."

In the end five kid's died and ten of them were expelled, one of them was Ojay and none of us ever heard of him again. I guess he was sent to one of those freedom school's, where they can do everthing they really like, and that's including living in a world full of music.

On wedesday we decided we'd go vist Rocky and Daltyboy in the joint.

Veronica was still pretty angry at Rocky for haveing been arested by the cop's in the first place, and I guess really, Seasonn would have been the same if Daltyboy was arested when she was around. Well in some way's that's what girlfreind's and boyfreind's are for, to tell each other's what's good, what's bad, what's right and what's wrong.

We sat waiting in the visitor's room for about fourty minute's before one of the warder's finally came and told us that we could go in, but not all together. It made me wonder why they had such thing's as visitor's hour's, when freind's could'nt all go in at the same time. But then I thought we could see our freind's.

Veronica went in first to see Rocky and I went in first to see Dalty boy. He looked rather gloomy and tired as we sat talking to each other's behind the little glass window, but he kind of looked surprized too when I told him about the school riot.

"Hey what was it like?" He asked. "Was it something worse than the maffia squad or something more out of a comedy show?"

"Something more out of a maffia squad." I decieded. "It was worse than world war two actuallly."

"Hey did anybody get bumped off?"

"Yes Mr. Odessy." My voice was slightly weak. "And about five other kid's."

"That's bad." Said Daltyboy. "Really, really bad because Mr. Odessy was my best buddy, you know that he was one of the greatest's teacher's that I've ever known." Daltyboy's face went suddenly meanly hard and I watched as he pulled his finger's through his hair.

"Do you know who the ring leader was – and was it somebody that I knew only too well?"

"He was in our class, Ojay Wargacki, the one with the black hair and he wear's tatoo's on his arm's."

"Is he still in our class?" Daltyboy's voice was anxoius.

"No I think he's been expelled from the school."

"You – think."

"He has."

"Aw that's too bad, cause I would've rammed my finger's right down his throat, if he was around when I got myself outta this mess."

"Really?" I said not beleiveing for once that Daltyboy would ever commit such a callous murder.

"Yeah really – and that's the truth, cause he was a nut and Mr. Odessy was my greatest teacher."

I smiled and noded my head. "Yes and he was one of my greatest teacher's too."

I was talking to Rocky fifteen minute's after that and he looked just as gloomy and tired as Dalty boy had.

"Hey they make you do every single thing under the sun in this godemed lousy place." He said. "And man can I wait to get out."

"And when's that going to be?" I asked.

"When ever I can, and that's gonna be fast."

"Did Veronica tell you any about the school riot?"

Rocky nodded his head. "But all I need now is some of that Marijuana this place is like a cemertry, and I need some enlightment."

"Have you much left?"

"I don't know, but I do know for sure that my parent's are gonna really have me kicked out the house this time, their not gonna put up with it if they know that I've been aressted and that I'm high on drug's."

"Well, that's better than been in the joint." I exclaimed.

"Yeah but where do I go?"

I shrugged my shoulder's. "How's your arm, okay?"

"Okay, but they could have left the bandaged off and have me bleed to death insted, cause like I said this place is just like a cemertry and no matter what happen's I'm gonna find myself outta here more than fast."

They did'nt come out for about another three week's and in that time Seth, Veronica and I just lived for today and tomorrow. Sometime's I would ask myself what am I doing with my life? Where am I headed? And that made me feel less of myself. I suddenly thought why, the disco, why the school riot and why Seasons death, and why now this?

We all played hooky for most of those week's, and I think my mother knew because she kept makeing suspicous glance's at me when ever I came in from roaming around town, or going to the movie house with Seth and Veronica. That's all we did actually and we spent about four dollar's buying chip's, drink's and ciggerate's. Somehow Rocky's marijuana had grown on us, but then when he came out of the joint he changed on takeing L.S.D, and just like he had done with the marijuana he made us take it too.

"Hey what are these?" Seth asked. Rocky had just placed some colorful pill's onto the palm's of our hand's and told us to eat them. They were so small that we could hardly vizulize them.

"Just eat them." Said Rocky smiling. We watched as he held back his head, sending a mountain of pill's into his mouth.

Seth after a while gave up and did the same, so did Veronica and Dalty boy, then finally I shrugged my shoulder's and ate the pill's as well.

By the time we got into the automobile, I was haveing an assortment of crazy mindblowing hallucination's.

There must have been at lest a dozon pink elephant's roaming around outside as Rocky started up the engine and sped around the corner. Sometime's I thought we were in the orange mustang and other time's I could see that we were been chased hysterically by a whole moutain of red and green spotted cranefly's. I closed my eye's and they were still there, I buried my face into Veronica's jacket and they were still there, I finally pressed my hand's tightly over my eye's and for the love of god, they were still there.

Veronica was yelling out something and laughing like crazy as she pointed out of the window. "Have you ever seen yellow gorilla's before, well look there they are thousand's of them."

I could'nt see anything, except the five thousand, red and green, spotted cranefly's, and I wonderd what Seth and the other's were seeing right now.

"Help I can't move my feet." Seth yelled almost scsreaming. "I can't move their stuck – their stuck in this red, thick jelly, hey maybe you can help me out Rocky, hey Rocky."

Rocky was swerving around like a madman, his action's were fast and the mustang shook us around crazily like an earth tremor.

"There's about fifteen million white animal's headed our way and I don't know where to put this thing."

"Hey there's something right behind us." Yelled Daltyboy pointing franticly through the back window. "And Look I think it has bright red eye's help it's gonna kill us." Daltyboy was hysterical with fear and I was knocked flying onto Veronica as he scrambled like mad onto the floor.

When I turned back round to face the front we were no longer where ever we were, but we were someplace like paridise. It was a fantasic colorful picture of pink tree's, an orange sky and a beautiful mound of turquise grass. "Hey everybody is'nt this beautiful?" I anounced. "Is'nt this just like been in a beautiful widespread rainbow, hey Veronica you think it's nice too?"

Veronica said notthing, but was gapeing through the window with such a horrified experission that I thought she must be seeing some thing that I was'nt seeing, and whatever it was I did'nt want to see it either.

Then I turned to the front and could have died. We were no longer been driven around by Rocky. It was something like out from a horror movie, yellow spidery apearance and a head like an over grown gauliflower.

"Seth." I yelled. "Where's Rocky?"

Seth turned around and his face was all blue and coverd in red spot's. "Olivia what are you getting at, Rocky's right here beside me and everbodie's enjoying the ride alright."

No I was'nt at that moment I could've sworn, I was wakening up into a jungle full of slithery, slimy yellow spotted snake's and spider's.

I was haveing one of those nightmare's where every crazy thing seemed to be comming from the oposite direction's, and I thought oh my god would I ever get out of it. My eye's were closed, but then wherever I turned my head, they were still there.

Flying through the air we were been chashed by every living form, every single five winged creature and every other spotted color, when suddenly I found my self been hurled toward the window. There was this big spinning explosion, somebody screamed, somebody was falling on top of me and everthing went summarly black.

We wer'nt in the mustang when we finally woke up. We were inside of a big white building. My arm was in a banaged and it ached with an excessive pain. Then something told me that we were in a hospital and that it was in a joint hospital.

"So young lady, your awake are you?"

I looked up and my eye's met those of an orderly. She had black, greying hair and the expression on her face was'nt actually one that could be described as a smile.

"What happened?" I asked. Sounding rather calm.

"What happened." The orderly seemed quite surprized as she went to open one of the white rimmed window's. "Just about everything that could happen in a night I reckon."

"What do you mean?" My head was in a state of perpetual confusion. The orderly stepped away from the window, her hands resting on her hip's as she stood preplxed over my bed.

"Honney, don't you know what happened?" Her voice was suddenly slow and serious. I shook my head.

"Then before I tell you, I'd better give you an injection." The orderly was about to make her way toward a small, needle conveying trolly when I called her back. "No waite, please, tell me what happened."

"Are you sure?"

I smiled weakly. "Yes do."

"Well what the report said was that you and your three freind's were last night involved in an auto wreck, it happened along the motor way and – you smashed into an on comeing pick up truck carrieing a family of four."

"Was... was anybody hurt?" My voice was almost a gasp.

"All of them were killed instantly."

"My... my freind's?"

"No, those beautiful little children and there parent's, there was two of them, they were so inocent and so were those young parent's." The orderly seemed romote. "Though there was no pain."

I sank back in to the pillow. My heart struck by lightening and my heart releived from sudden fear. "Did – my – freind's – my....."

"No, they all survived, and I can tell you their lucky that they did. Only a few broken bone's that's all." The orderly raised her eyebrow's. Then put her hand's back on her hip's. "And you'll all be fit enogh to vist the joint, by the end of the week. It's a sorry story whern thing's like this happen, but I know they ca'nt be help." My eye's were blurred by sudden tear's and the orderly walked away, then my mind was spinning into another world.

We were flying high with L.S.D. We were haveing fun, fun, fun, Rocky was in the driver seat and we were haveing the joyride of our life's. Color's were everywhere. Then it happened. I don't know what happened. What's happening to me? To us? Why did it have to happen? They were so inocent. We did'nt mean to kill them. To become J.D's for some thing that was'nt meant to happen. But it did happen and now we'll be all over the new's paper's. "Teen-age gang kill family of four. In a massive motorway autowreck." I closed my eye's. But how did we come to be on the motorway. Rocky must have somehow jumped onto it while he was trying to avoid those white colored animal's. We can blame it on the L.S.D., but one thing's for sure, I'm never going to use it again.

The cell block was almost brand new. I was in cell number two and I smoked two ciggerate's before trying to eat the meal that was layed out infront of me. I sat down on the bunk again. It was flat and the mattress was thinly hard. A grey comforter was the only thing that coverd it. We had to share a cell.

Another girl and I because all the other cell's were already as jam packed as a bee hive could be. She was sleeping up on the top bunk and when I came in she told me her name was Pricilla Slocum.

"Hi, what are you in here for honney?" She asked handing me a ciggerate. I shrugged my shoulder's. "The usual. Why are you in?"

"Hey c'mon I asked first?" She laughed. "You look to young to be a baddie and beside's I've been in for almost a year now."

"What have you been doing, to be kept in here so long?" I asked.

"I have'nt actually been in here for a year, I've been in and out of this garbage bin just like a yo-yo and it's all because I love mugging people."

"Oh." I said. She lit my ciggerate, then came down to sit beside me on my bunk. "How old are you?"

"Have a guess honney."

"Eighteen, nineteen."

"Wow, thank's for the compliment, I've been out of my teenage year's for as long as I can remember."

I studied her brown mass of tangled hair, her heartshaped face and her brown twinkling eye's. "You don't look more than eighteen."

"Well I'm twenty two and I'm still a virgin, baby how'd you dig that."

She laughed as she put her arm around my shoulder. "Say baby have you any dumb boyfreind's yet, anyway's how old are you?"

"Fifteen." I took another drag of my ciggerate.

"Your kidding and your in this dump already."

"Yes, and it's only because we were high on drug's. I and my freind's were in an auto wreck."

"Wow did any body get bumped off?"

"Mmm," I nodded my head. "They were inocent. There was four of them and they were in a pick up truck, we did'nt mean to... kill them though, it was an accident... Rocky was the driver. He was the one who decided we should have a joy ride, and when we did we were all of us high on L.S.D and was I seeing some hallucinations."

My mother had the aspect of fatigued disbeleive when I came out to see her in the visitor's room. She was'nt smiling or doing any thing she was just sitting there stareing blankly into space.

"Hello, mom." I said as I sat behind the glass window. "How's Oscar okay?"

She turned her head and looked at me slowly. "How could you Olivia, it was something that was never you, I don't know what to say. Just look at you Fiffteen and already in this place, your brother's never been in so why you?"

I shrugged my shoulder's. "It just happened, it was'nt our fault though, we only wanted a bit of fun."

"The only fun you'll be getting is at your aunt's house young lady, I'm not putting up with it any longer, you and your wreckless careless freind's, they don't do anything but drag you into trouble, first the disco and no this. Olivia I am sending you to your aunt's house and that is final."

I looked around and tried to say something agreeable. "Mom, their my best freind's, and what about my education, I've got some exam's comeing up in September."

"Never mind about school Olivia, I'm talking about your life. Your father died so tragicly and I'm not haveing you die the same way, with this kind of life your leading your bound to be dragged into an early, unessary death, and Olivia I don't want that to happen to you, or your brother."

My mind floated back to the time when my father had died. I suddenly tried to remember what my life was like then. It was exactly the same as it was now. Disco's, freind's, late night's and freguently playing hooky. Maybe I thought. This is me. The real Olivia Englewood, of the disco world. The kid who love's to be a disco queen, and flaunt of her talent's to the whole outside world. I could just see myself starting my life all over again. In exactly the same, wild, exciting way. Maybe my life will be like this for the rest of my crazy, hectic day's, Seth, Veronica, Daltyboy and Rocky. Their me. Their all a part of me.

"And Olivia you don't fool me by playing hooky all day, or by your new found desire for takeing drug's. How could you Olivia it's murder for me. Your behavoir is getting me right down. Your beginning to seem both stupid and iresponsible. What would your father say if he could see you now. Destroying your life when you should be stepping out and starting it fresh like when I was around your age. I don't know Olivia your just beyond reality, forever floating around on cloud nine."

I shrugged my shoulder's. Trying not to look too argreeable with what my mother was saying. Beside's it was all true. My life is just like that happy and free. "Maybe I could try and come down mom. Destroy my way of living now and start all over again." But still I knew I would never do that.

"Now your talking sense Olivia, and that's the way I expect any daughter of mine to talk. You may be tried in court for that disasterous auto wreck, and for you been high on drug's but when it's over it's back to me again, then over to your aunt's house for some rest. So you can say goodbye to your freind's for a while I can tell you. No more disco's no more late night's and no more drug's is that understood?"

I shook my head trying to imagine what it would be like living without my life. Without Seth, without Veronica, without Daltyboy and without Rocky. It would be murder I thought as I said goodbye to my mother and slowly made my way back to my cell.

We were all find 200 dollar's for careless, under aged driveing and for processing an automobile while under the act's of drug's, also with the fact that it was stolen. We all came out but Rocky was put under probation for a year. Then his father savagagly done him over and that was that we'd all up and run away.

I did'nt care what my mother would think or my brother, but it was Seth who really pushed me into doing it. When I told him about my mother's plan's for me he suddenly went as dead as a do-do and told me arubtly that he woidld rather bump himself off that see me fly the coop. I knew that I was pressured by his love, so I simply forgot about my planned future and thought about another one, instead.

We went to the disco that night, Seth, Veronica, Daltyboy and Rocky and I. That is before we said goodbye to our house's for the last time. It was hot inside as usall. The music was blareing and the kid's were dancing crazy. Michale Jackson's "liveing of the wall" pounded through Seth's and mine ear's as we hustled energeticly to the sound of the beat, and I thought lucidly that is just what we'd be doing in a matter of day's. Makeing life easy. Better start before we get too old. Sure it made sense. It's something everybody should think of once in a while.

We danced like mad for three hour's. My eye's were dazzling by my guessing so were Seth's I could see as he swerved around like a disco king. He reached out his arm's toward me, his sliver chain swinging crazliy about his neck. He is'nt actually hunky dory when it come's to dancing, but then he has some pretty weird antic's on doing it his own way. He think's that if you like music you should let it like you too, by dancing to it as much as you can no matter how crazy you dance to it.

There were kid's everywhere though, doing the freak. They spread their leg's, bent their knee's and advanced upon each other's untill they finally got to touching each other.

As we were dancing I saw Daltyboy once flashing in the crowd, he was doing the freak with another guy and it looked as though they were both truly enjoying theirself's. I signalled them out to Seth and he just shrugged his shoulder's as he made a funny face. I shrugged my shoulder's too, thinking it has to be a gay life, and prolonged with my energetic dancing.

The whole of the disco club was fully absorbed by the stenrian music and the crazy dancing hustle's. When somebody, somewhere suddenly made a brawl and all hell broke lose. There were kid's everywhere stabbing at each other.

Sozzled girl's still crazily dancing or doing the freak with their partner's. Then the D.J was yelling out over the music. "Hey C'mon everybody let's keep the harmoney going, there's no time for crazy fighting, but there is time for a whole lotta groovy dancing so c'mon let's see y'all dance – C'mon everybody dance." Everybody ignored him, but somebody was turning frenzie at his sudden outburst of word's and I saw as he was dragged down from the balcony, along with some other D.J's and reapeatly stabbed as they all tried to push of some of the crazy kid's.

There kid's everywhere doing crazy antic's of pill popping as they shimmyed to the beat of the hottest, powerful music, in the disco. I was showerd suddenly by a whole mountain full of colored pill's as everybody shuffled around wildly, some popping pill's other's killing for the fun of it.

Seth and I were jostled around scurrliously like tennis ball's in a court yard. I could see that he was beginning to lose his cool. I suddenly wonderd why we ever came here if it was going to end up like this. Then I rememberd my mother's word's. "Never mind about schooll Olivia, I'm talking about your life."

Seth summarly swung around, butting somebody on his nose as the offender like a maniac tried to knife him with his blade. They struggled tremendously for a full two minute's. I frantcly called out his name each time I thought he was going to lose. Seth won, he floored the maniac. He grabbed my hand then we both struggled to get to the front.

The whole place was an uproar as cop's stormed, armed with gun's into the building. They barcaded the entrance as raging kid's wrestled with them like posioned snake's. Loud bullet whiz's was the only sound to be heard together with the sound of bellowing music.

"This is a drug raid, we shoot to kill if nobody corroperate's." A cop yelled.

His voice was something like an echoe. Everbody stopped. "We want you all to come out slowly, with your hand's raised, no messing about just be nice."

There was a shout from the crowd. Somebody ran out and we saw as he tore of his jacket, throwing it to the floor. Somebody eles did the same, then everbody tore of their jacket's doing the same thing. They stepped back in silence all refuseing to co-operate with the cop's. "You'll have to bust us first – you lousy fuck headed creep's." The boy yelled as he kicked his jacket flying to one of the cop's. "So start shooting, pig's."

One of the cop's slowly put his gun back into his holster, as he signalled to some more cop's outside. His face was suddenly overcome.

"Okay, then you have it all your own way."

There was a big commotion as though the roof was caveing in. I looked up to see the black of the night stareing through with a blanket of gleaming star's.

The cop's were up there. I figured they were trying to get in. Then there was this big dramatic sound of something been sprayed.

Seth and I looked up to see a gigantic hose been lowered into the building.

A moment passed. All hell broke lose as kid's everywhere made a stampead. There was something like fire stinging my eye's. I grabbed hold of Seth. My eye's were growing dim it was like a whole pot of salt had suddenly been thrown in my face. Kid's were pulling up their jacket's to cover their eye's. Seth was saying something that I could'nt hear because of this deafening sound which was now racking my ear's as well as my eye's.

"Hey everybody they have tear gas." Yelled somebody. "These pig's have got it made."

Tear's streamed down my face. Hot with fire. Seth was bandageing his eye's with the sleeve of his jacket. He yelled out to me. "Olivia we have to get outta here." I felt myself been pulled toward the entrance. We were suddenly hit my a mountain full of tear gas comming from the oposite direction. My eye's had just been attacked by a swamp of jellyfish. Seth let go of my hand. Kid's were screaming everywhere. He was out of my reach. I called out to him. I heard him call back to me. Then we were together again. "Seth, how do we.. get out of here?" I heard myself yell. There was no reply except the feeling that I was been dragged over a whole row of bodie's. They were dead I suddenly thought, even though I did'nt like to think they were. Somebody was yelling it was one of the cop's. "Okay, now all of you get your ass's outta here and this time there's gonna be no messing around, you understand?"

I could'nt see a thing. I was like a robut with my hand's sticking out in front of me. Seth had let go of me again. I grabbed the end of his jacket. We ambled out into the cool night air like camel's in a desert. The cop's were behind us all pushing us out. I had the jumpy feeling that one of them was sticking a gun into my back. Then we were all lined up against the building. My eye's were getting back to normall by then. So were Seth's I guessed, though I could'nt be sure.

I wiped the tear's away. People from all over had come to see the trouble.

I knew that Seth was trying to make a run for it. He was getting summarly restless. Then I saw her. It was my mother I'm sure it was. Were my eye's honestly deceiveing me? "Seth" I whisperd. "I think my mother's here, she's standing in the crowd.." My eye's widened slghtly. "And look I can see Oscar as well, he's on his motorbike."

"Who the hell's Oscar?" Asked Seth forgetting that he was only my brother.

"My brother." I said. "But come on what are we going to do?"

"Your not going back home, that's for sure." Seth was almost yelling. "Were getting outta here – and that's now."

There was notthing that I could do. Notthing that I wanted to do except run. We made ourselve's risk the danger of getting ourselve's shot to death by the cop's. As we ran I was suddenly torn between two love's. It was either Seth or my mother. My mother, my brother or my lover. I suddenly stopped. Seth pulled me on. Then I knew that he was for me. Without me I knew that he would die.

There were real tear's in my eye's as I rememberd the sad look of my mother's anguised face. She was standing there under the black starlit sky with Oscar. It all seemed so eeirly unreal.

We ran on until we reached the corner of the building. There were parent's everywhere grabbing hold of their kid's, angerly pulling them into waiting automobils or just clean away from the maddening, crazy, cop infested building.

Seth was wild with anxiety by the times we had skidded to a stop. He ran his hand's through his hair like crazy. "C'mon where are they." he yelled. "We alway's get outta there before they do, hey you know something, this is worse than waiting for the high-school bus, it's worse than..." His word's were suddenly cut short by the angry roar of a motorcycle. We both turned around to see my brother thundering through the air after us. I suddenly could'nt beleive that Oscar was so good at rideing that bike. He was so fast. Seth and I had hardly any time to run, before he was right ontop of us.

I could'nt tell who was the angret, Seth or him. Then I knew it was Seth.

He suddenly swung around as though he'd been hit. then he was glareing at Oscar as though his greatest desire was to kill him. "Hey listen big brother, she's with me alright." Then I watched as he smiled slightly. "Don't worry cause were gonna take good care of each other."

"Olivia, c'mon you have to come home." Oscar was just egnoring Seth he looked as though he wanted me to get on the back of his bike.

"Mom's... waiteing for you down the front."

I looked around not quite knowing what to say or do. There was a black, heavy silence in which Oscar looked at me, Seth looked at him.

"Hey Oscar, she's a big girl now you know?"

"Where were you heading just now anyway's?" Oscar asked still forgetting that Seth was there.

"No where special, just walking." I replyed, trying to sound nonchant.

"Hey Oscar what do you want?" Seth sounded meaner.

"I came to get my sister, and she's comming back with me." I watched as Oscar got of his bike, putting down the stand with his foot.

"No, you have'nt because your gonna get back on your beloved bike and roar right back down the ally on it."

"Oh yeah, and who's gonna make me?"

Seth was starting toward him, I knew there was going to be a fight.

"I am and so you are gonna fly the coop." Seth was on top of him before Oscar had time to do anything. I yelled out horrified for them to stop. They fought like mad, falling to the ground as they both tried to beat each other to a pulp.

"Seth." I yelled, there was the sound of running feet. I swung around to see three dark figure's running toward us. I knew who they were. My heart was suddenly relived from fright. At my feet Seth and Oscar were still trying to maime each other. I watched anxiously as both Daltyboy and Rocky helped to pull them apart.

There was a tremedous struggle then Oscar was getting back onto his bike. His face was coverd in a mass of blood and bruise's. Seth was still glareing at him, as he looked at me with his patheict sad eyes, cockle spanial look. "You'll be sorry about this sis, these are crazy kid's, mom's doing her nut, she's never gonna forgive you either." He started up his motorcycle, roaring back down the ally on it. I stared after him for sometime. Seth put his arm's around me. His expression seemed guilty under the gleam of the bright star's.

"Hey, listen, Livvy – christ I'm sorry, I did'nt even give you a chance – it's up to you." His arm's slipped away from me. "Go after him if you like, I don't mind, I won't love you any lesser than I do now."

My eye's met those of Veronica's, Daltyboy's and Rocky's. They seemed to be anxousily, solem under the darkness of the sky. My heart was pounding with sudden pain. This was something that I had to decided. It was to be the discisson of my life. Slowly I gazed into Seth's eye's. I rememberd the first time we'd met. He smiled slightly. This had to be the discison.

"Listen everybody." I said. "You don't need to look so glum, because I'm staying right where I am." There was a loud yell of joy from them all. Veronica lept up into the air. She hugged me like crazy, untill I could no longer vizulize the bright star's.

"This is something I knew you'd say." She laughed. "We could never do without you Olivia."

Rocky and Daltyboy were just as crazy. They were hugging me so hard that I thought my bone's would break. "Glad to have you back Livvy, love is the word that keep's everybody together." Yelled Rocky. "And we sure do love you, and that's for life."

I looked around. Seth was standing behind me all looking a little bit dazed.

He was pointing to something that I could'nt quite see. Then I realized that he was pointing to Daltyboy. Daltyboy's ear. "Hey, Seth what's the matter?" Rocky yelled. "What's the matter with Daltyboy?"

"I don't know, but he's got this great chunk of his ear missing." Seth went up to him. I stared in horror at what I saw. Daltyboy's erring had just been violently ripped out. His whole lobe was a blood coverd mess.

"Hey, guy's come on I know I'm not that good looking, so why rub me as though you wanna marry me." Said Daltyboy. He did'nt even know what his ear was doing. It was bleeding like mad.

"Daltyboy your earring has just been ripped out." Yelled Seth. "And your ear has just been torn to thread's."

Daltyboy shrugged his shoulder's, touching his ear. Then he almost jumped out of his skin. "Wow, hey your right. My precious earing has just flown the coop."

"Hey what happened back there?" Rocky asked. We all watched as Daltyboy shrugged his shoulder's again. Then he looked as though he was crying.

"I don't know kid's, – but – I think I've just – killed a guy."

"You what?" Yelled Seth. "You THINK you've just killed a GUY?"

"Yeah – and man I – did'nt – mean too, you know it was – just an accident." Daltyboy was really crying now. He was shakeing like a leaf as he sat down on the sidewalk, his head in his hand's.

"Hey wait a minute are you sure you killed somebody, was it inside of that disco?" Seth asked. We were all of us struck by lightening. How could we believe that our best buddy, Daltyboy had just killed somebody?

"Yeah it was in the – disco, and we were only fighting – then this guy pull's out a blade and threaten's to knife me with it – and hey man I did'nt mean to kill him."

"It's Okay." Said Seth. "Just tell us how you got to kill him."

"Look – I just killed him alright I grabbed the blade and stuck it in his chest, he deid because his eye's were wide open and when I touched him he – did'nt move."

Daltyboy suddenly stood up, looking around wildly as though he could hear something. His eye's were wide and frightened. I thought he must have gone crazy with nerve's. Seth went over to put an arm around his shoulder. Even then he jumped.

"Hey listen Dalty, if you really killed a guy, really really killed a guy then we have to split." Seth was already beginning to amble down the street. I glanced at Veronica and she glanced at Rocky. We all ran after him. Then ran back to Daltyboy. He was wipeing his eye's. "Listen everybody I don't care what you say, but I'm giving myself up."

"Hey, no c'mon." Yelled Rocky. "That ain't fair is it, I mean look, there were hundred's of kid's inside of that disco just killing anybody and are they gonna turn themselve's into those goddemed cop's, no there not and so why you huh, that's dumb."

Daltyboy was hastily shakeing his head. "No, I feel like some crimnal and I wanna get it all over with."

I put my arm around his shoulder. "Listen Daltyboy, were all going now and nobodie's going to find you, okay?"

"No, look you all listen, I don't feel right alright." Daltyboy was backing away all the time, carefully as though he were walking backward's on a plank. "And I don't wanna be branded as a hideaway for the rest of my life now do I, so understand this kid's, I'm doing it for the best." He took one turn and ran down the street. In a moment Seth and Rocky were straight after him. Seth reached him first bringing him down like a rugby player.

Veronica was yelling out, jumping up and down like a cheerleader. "Hurray, hurray. We don't wanna lose Daltyboy now do we?"

I agreed with her too. Rooting loudly as they all came back. When Daltyboy got back into the circle. We did everything as much as we could to persuade him to stay with us. He just looked at us all for a while. Then he shrugged his shoulder's. "Okey, alright you got me. So I won't turn myself in. I'll stay by you all and up and run away with you. I know that those freind's of the guy I killed are gonna be after my blood any moment, so what are we waiting for let's all fly the coop."

It was the longest, most senseibleest speech I'd ever heard Daltyboy say. It was the happiest, most unforgettable night in my life as all of us all with an arm around a shoulder ambled down the ally. This was the road to freedom. The road that I had been waiting for, for so long. No it was happening. Now we were together, and we would alway's be together. Seth, Veronica, Daltyboy and Rocky. Forever. It was truly going to be a night for us all to remember. The star's shone down, their message's of goodbye's. The moon shone down it's moon light of good luck, and the dark ebonny sky showered down it's blanket full of happiness, peacefullest and over flowing goodwill. I was smileing as we all turned out of the ally into the main street. So were the other's. Because we were all happy, and we were all free.

The truck trailer that we had finally tried to flag down pulled up at a nearby signpost. He was a burly, beefy man of around thirty eight. With large dark busy eyebrow's, small black deep set eye's and a dark rough unshaved complexion. "Okay." He said. "Where you headed?" We made up some kind of effort to suggest a place then shrugged our shoulder's. "Anywhere's." Seth said finally.

"Okay kid's anywhere's it'll be, jump in." He pushed open the side door, letting us all somehow squash in to the front seat. I sat beside the window with Veronica.

Seth, Rocky and Daltyboy had all managed to get in first. Though I did'nt care because right now I was feeling happy, warm and relaxed.

"Hey where did you kids spring from?" The truck driver had already started up the engine, we were on the highway. he looked around at us all for a moment. "Have you all any home's?"

"Yeah, were just going someplace." Said Seth sounding nonchanlt.

"Your just going someplace." Laughed the truck driver. "That's the worst joke I've everd herd in ma life. Hey now c'mon kid's what are you really huh, runaway's?"

The question made me wake up slightly.

"No we just dig travelling." Rocky said. "And we dig hitching lift's."

"Aw you do, well I can give you a line, you've picked the right truck tonight kid's, and whereever your headed your bound to get there with me."

"What are you doing now night shift?" Asked Seth sounding suddenly important.

"Naw, I'm headed home now, to my hotel somewhere's around San Diego, and I'll be there in less than awhile now, why? You wanna stop in with me?" He paused and looked at us. "Just for the night eh?"

"We don't mind sleeping rough." Daltyboy glanced through the side window. The driver looked down at his tee-shirt curiously. "Hey your coverd in blood, what you bin doing killing a pig?"

I was thinking Daltyboy would tell him about the disco. There was a short silence. He shrugged his shoulder's, then rubbed his hand's down over his tee-shirt. "I guess red is my fravoite color."

"Huh." The driver laughed. "What's your name kid?"

"Dalton, but my freinds call me Daltyboy."

I could tell that Daltyboy was beginning to get a little subconouis. He was'nt actually talking so happy.

"Well, Daltyboy you ought'nt to be sleeping around rough at your age. I mean all of you ought'nt to be sleeping rough cause your all growing and growing kid's ought'nt to damage their health like that."

I thoght he sounded rather parental now. Like my father. But something was missing. I was just like doing a jigsawpuzzle, you can't find one more single peice when you know it has to be found.

"Yeah, well we dig sleeping rough." Emphized Rocky.

"Yeah well what about the girl's then?"

"What about us?" Veronica exclaimed in a sqeaky voice.

"Okay kid's." The driver glanced around at our blank face's. "So you don't wanna come and stay for the night, okay then just lay back, relaxe, just imagine that your biteing into a succulent roast duck with all the wine to drown you in the world." The driver glanced at us again, grinning. "For all a you huh? Nice warm bed's to sleep in when your tuckerd. and some nice cuddely teddy-bear's for the girl's to cuddle, now aint that just great." He laughed. "No sleeping around in my place I kin tell you." He looked at us again still laughing.

We all looked around at each other with blank expression's. Seth's eye's met mine. I was thinking I knew what he was going to say. It had to be all of that luxury, that the driver described.

"Your on." He said.

"That's great." The driver smiled at him. "That's really great." I guess we were all glad because it would mean a real bed for the night and a real kind of meal. I smiled as Seth looked at me. He looked at the other's, they all nodded their head's and Rocky gave him a thumb's up sign. "That's sense man."

We were off the highway in about another two hour's. I was feeling pretty tierd by then. I guessed Veronica was too. She was yawning like crazy by the time we were shown into the apartment. Maybe the truck driver was a smart guy, or maybe he's just good at telling root-back's, because we could'nt see anything in the apartment that was actually luxiourious, when we gott here.

"Okay boy's and girl's make yourself's at home, cause this is where I live." It was'nt as though he was expecting us to notice anything, but everything around the place was dark, cold and damp. I looked at Seth and he shrugged his shouder's. Rocky was even more curious. He scratched his head as he razed his eyebrow's. "Hey, listen this dos'nt look like the kind of apartment that anybody would spend the night in."

"Hey listen kid, just shaddup will you." The driver did'nt seem to be laughing anymore. He sounded as though he had just woken up. "This, all this is for free, and you don't have to pay one single little cent. You understand, so just relaxe huh." He smiled again slowly, breaking into a grin.

I shrugged my shoulder's. "Where's all the succulent roast duck and red wine?" There was no such aroma of any luxiourous meal.

"Go and help yourself make some cawfee if yah dig." The driver opened up another door. "It's right on in there, go on make yourself feel nice."

"Okay." I smiled. "C'mon Veronica." She came with me into the squild, what was susposed to be a luxorious kitchen. It was pretty small and the greyish, brown wall's had faint trace's of steam running down them.

I tried to find some suitable cup's. Veronica came up with a few rusty looking one's. "Gee – this place is no hotel." She breathed. "It look's more like a goldmine."

I nodded my head as I studied the pigsty of a place. "I wonder how anybody can just say that they live here and like it."

"Well I don't. It's just like the joint." Veronica tried to turn on one of the faucet's. I went over to help her when it did'nt look as though it was going to move. We finally got it to work, then I was thinking it can't be that bad if somebody actually live's here, and can survive.

The truck driver studied us all as we sat in the lounge. It's wall's were coverd in all sort's of black and white photograph's. They were various picture's of solnem faced boy's. In one of the picture's a boy with long blonde hair wore an earing. I drank my jarva thinking the truck driver must have a lot of son's, though not one of them resembled him. "Well, kid's howd you feel? Okay? Why don't you all tell me what your name's are, your birth sign's are and how old you all are?"

"That's alot of information i's'nt it?" Seth laughed.

"Why, don't you dig the fuzz?" The truck driver began to laugh too. I was wondering if he would find out what my zodiac sign was by guessing. Well been an Aire's, born on 16th April I guess I can call myself ambitous, active, carefree and mostly extrovert, with my perfect complexion, lean prominent face and a weird shaped, tawny haired head.

The truck driver was studeing Seth evenly for a moment then he snapped his finger's. "Yeah I gocth yah. Your a scorpion ain't you?"

Seth nodded his head. He was surprized. "Yeah you got me, I'm a scorpio actually, but I don't care much for zodiac sign's anyway's."

"Okay now, so how old are you all?"

"Were all teen-aged." Seth said putting down his cup. He looked around at us all smiling.

"Oh yeah, and you all look it too. You all got such nice soft skin." The truck driver ran his hand across his rough surface. "And I don't only mean the girl's I mean the boy's aswell." He laughed penitrateingly for a while. I took another swig of my jarva.

"Hey kid you like the picture's then?"

I nodded my head as he looked at me. "Yes their nice, all of them. Are they your kid's?"

His eye's blinked slightly, as he ran his hand around the back of his neck swiftly. "Naw, naw they ain't ma kid's. I did'nt even have enough time to get married. Their just freind's. Good freind's yah know. Their the one's who kept me going sometime's. When it was bad like."

I saw as he fouced his eye's lucidly on the picture with the dark background, and long blonde haired boy. His eye's looked as though they were trying to read something. Then he turned back to us, his eye's resting firmly on Daltyboy. "Hey you know kid your gonna get some posion into that cut of your's if you don't go get it mended. Why'nt you take a trip to the bathroom and make it look nicer." He was looking at Daltyboy's ripped ear, and I was figuring he already knew that some thing was missing.

Daltyboy shrugged his shoulder's. "It's okay now, it's not hurting me anymore."

"Hey, now c'mon it will be hurting you if you don't go and tend to it now." The truck driver talked seriously. "It's gonna go all septic and then your gonna lose an ear. You don't want that now do you?"

Daltyboy shook his head. "No, I guess not."

"Then I guess you'd better get to that bathroom." The truck driver finalized.

"Maybe I ought to go with him." Veronica said as she stood up. "He'll be needing somebody to help with the washing and the creameing."

"Okay you go help him." The truck driver nodded his head. "And you'll find plenty of that soothing creme in the cabinate."

As they left the room I was thinking would they ever succeed in finding the bathroom in this crazy apartment, further more the cabinate and the soothing creme. The truck driver gazed after them for a moment. Then he looked at Seth and Rocky. His eye's studied them both for a good two minute's, slowly and carefully. "Hey, you know something I could alway's tell that one of your were a scorpio," He pointed to Seth shrewdly. "Because you have it in your eye's, they look cool and stinging, hey did you know that your actually lucky to have them eye's? They make you look different from other kid's, and I like kid's who look different."

Seth nodded his head slightly with a smile. "You do?"

"I do, hey you know something I actually find you both good looking. I find you both sexy, know what I mean?"

I could hardely beleive what he was saying. Neither could Seth or Rocky.

We all just sat there silent for a while.

"In fact I find it easir to like boy's better then girl's." I watched skeptical as the truck driver put out his hand onto rest on Seth's knee.

"I just find you all beautiful."

Seth pushed his hand away. "Hey, what is this a call house?"

"No, it's not but I can give you anything, like I said everything is free no cent's but then how about another price?"

"I think we oughta go now." Rocky stood up. I did the same my eye's pleading over to Seth.

"No, all of you sid down, the girl can go. The boy's have got a deal."

"What kind of a deal?" I asked.

"None of your busness your just a girl." The truck driver stood up pushing Rocky back onto the divan. "You stay there, don't move."

"Hey you don't talk to her like that." Seth suddenly yelled.

"Kid if you yell like that once more I'm gonna break your ass off, you understand."

Seth stood up like crazy his face wild with anger. "Look you, I don't know what you are, but whatever it is I don't give a hang. Were just getting outta here right now and don't you try stopping us either."

I watched astouneded as the truck driver suddenly flung himself on to Seth, grabbing him like a maniac. "Now listen, baby your not going anywhere's, cause right now it's time for bed and beleive me you are."

Seth suddenly seemed to be under his spell. He went all calm. "Okay, okay, we can stay the night." He slowly pushed the truck driver away. "But don't ever do that again."

"That's great." Said the truck driver. "Really swell." He stepped back still studieing Seth.

I turned around to see Veronica and Daltyboy standing in the doorway.

Veronica had a weird look on her face. So did Daltyboy. "Hi." She said. "Were back."

The truck driver turned around. A grin on his face. "Okay now kid's it's time for bed, so why'nt I show you your room's huh?"

Daltyboy nodded his head slowly. I could tell that he knew something had just happened. He was looking at Seth and Rocky in such a revealing way. I smiled at Veronica trying to look normal.

"And I don't want you haveing any sex either." The truck driver sounded sly. "Cause if you do I'm gonna kick you out."

Seth and Rocky were looking at him as though he was some kind of maniac.

I was thinking the same thing too. He was altogether just an ordinary truck driver. We had thumbed a lift and we had got a lift. But now suddenly I was wishing we'd never left home. I was wishing that we had never thumbed that lift. Because we were here now and I knew that something strange was happening. I knew that this truck driver was no ordinary truck driver.

He looked at us hard for a moment with sapient eye's. Then he clicked his finger's. "Okay I'll have one of you boy's in with me. I want the one with the cut ear, because he's not gonna get so angry and put up a fight when I do nice thing's to him."

Daltyboy looked around at us motionless. The muscle's in his face were tensely rigid. "Hey, what's going on hear?" He looked across at the truck driver tetanusly.

"You heard Daltyboy, your in with me, so what's the stalling for?" The truck driver came over to him and put an arm around his shoulder. "Now C'mon I know you better than that, not to refuse an offer so good as mine."

Though we all knew Daltyboy was a homosexual he did'nt look as though he was getting sexually aroused by the truck driver. His eye's were cold. "That's a lie, you don't know a thing about me."

The truck driver laughed. "Well no need to get your pant's in a twist Daltyboy, cause we are gonna get to know each other and that's a truth."

He was still holding Daltyboy when he showed us to our room's. They were small empty and out of style. "Hey now don't worry girl's I'm not gonna steal your boy's from you just yet, so there's absoutely no reason for you to look so glum."

I felt as Seth slipped his arm around my waist. He was stareing around the room with cold, brittle eye's.

"But listen kid's I am gonna have you separated from each of your indivigual sex's. So that mean's, I want the boy's in one room and the girl's in the other. It's all because I don't want you having sex while your in my place, you understand?"

We nodded our head's slowly and I had the feeling that we were in a reformatory center.

Veronica and I both shared the big magoghany doble bed that was stationed in the center of the room. I was feeling kind of homesick and I was trying to imagine what it would be like if I was still at home in my own, big, warm bouncy bed. I had a sudden close up vision of myself as I wrote down the day's event's in my dairy. Then I summarly rememberd that I had forgotten it. I turned across to look at Veronica. She was sleeping. My heart was suddenly heavy with a deep regret. My mother would alway's be wondering why I went away without my beloved red dairy. Infact I had forgotton everything. My monney box, my hair brush (my hair was right now in tangle's), my tooth brush, my night dress and all my clothe's. I now realized that I was still wearing my blue jean's, my light turquise top and my white red rimmed sneaker's. Of course I had taken of my sneaker's, but I still felt a little odd as I fell asleep that night. It was probably because I was in a completely different room, a completely different bed and a completely different house. Or rather more – apartment.

I awoke to the sound of the truck driver's merry voice. "C'mon you kid's let's go get our selve's some of that beautiful breakfast." He was walking up the hallway banging on our door's, like as though there was some kind of dramatic fire. I sat up abrubtly. For a moment forgetting where exactly I was. Then I regonized Veronica's head of untidy titian colored hair as she slept with her arm's wrapped snugly around a pillow. I touched her slightly not actually wanting to disturb her slumber by awakeing her too suddenly. "Veronica." I whisperd. "It's morning and now we have to get out of here."

"Mmmm." She stirred slightly before dropping off into another round of snoreing. "Veronica." I stiffly climed out of the bed. Ambling toward the door and quitely opening it. All down the hallway it was empty. It rather reminded me of the time when I and my brother and my parent's had taken a pleasure trip on the Q.E.2. to Las Vegas and back. Oscar and I had been running up and down the corridor like two little monkey's by the time the trip was over. He was six and I was three so we can be exused I guess, but there did gome the time when the captain was going to throw us over board. We knew we wer'nt susposed to run up the corridor like that. Though we were only doing it for a little bit of fun, and I guess everybody need's a little fun on the boat.

Right now I was thinking on running up the hallway, wakeing up the boy's and getting the hell out of here. I was just planning on going when the sound of the truck driver's voice sounded. It came from the direction of the kitchen. I stepped back inside for a moment. Then nippieped lighltly along the hallway, to the door at the end.

I opened it slowly. Seth and Rocky suddenly sat up. They were already awake. "Hi there." I said. "C'mon WE have to get out of here."

"Aw why?" It was Seth who spoke. "I'm flattened out like a hound, and beside's we have'nt eaten a thing yet."

I stood skeptical in the doorway Rocky pulled of the comfortor's, leaping out of bed. "Yeah C'mon Seth she's right, we all have to get outta here – and now."

Seth slowly pulled back his mass of untidy dark hair. He yawned tierdly for a full four second's. Then got out of bed. "Yeah Livvy I'm as dead as a do-do. Let's get ourselve's moveing."

He ambled toward me slipping his arm around me. We ambled down the hallway back to our room to finally drag Veronica out from her sleep.

Then we went along the hallway to guessingly, the triuck driver's room. It was dark inside even though the drape's had been drawn and the sun light was peeking out. There was no sign of Daltyboy, but we went in anyway's. "Woe, is'nt it eerie in here." Said Veronica she went to stand by the window.

"Yeah, and heck it stink's of my dad's aftershave." Rocky let out a long, thin whistle.

Seth and I ambled over to a large bookcase. It was stacked with all kind's of magazine's and book's. "Hey give a look at this." Anounced Seth. "Our truck driver sure like's playboy magazine's don't he, and jesus he dig's kinky stuff too."

"Hey did you say kinky?" Rocky ambled over, helping himself to a magazine.

"Yeah, and I mean Kinky kinky." Said Seth. He waved the mag into the air. I was just flicking through some, when there was a noise at the doorway. The truck driver stalked in, a faint gleam of malice in his eye's. His face was not a pretty sight.

"Hey, what the damn hell do you kid's think your doing in here?" He flung the mag's from our hand's.

"Where not thinking of been in here, we are here." Seth proclaimed showing the palm's of his hand's, shrugging his shoulder's.

The truck driver glared at him. "You again you alway's make a brawl your mouth is too big for your head, now get out cause it's eat's."

I thought this whole episode was beginning to sound a little like goldie lock's and the three bear's. I was thinking the truck driver seemed a little over acted in what he did.

"I said C'mon now get out. And hey kid what is your name?" He looked at Seth with a currious expression before grabbing hold of his arm.

"My last name or my first name?"

"Your first name. Don't get nifty with me."

"Seth."

"Seth?"

"Yeah Seth. What's the matter don't you like it?"

"I love it, now c'mon let's get moveing."

The four of us along with the truck driver ambled slowly down the hallway. Veronica and I went first and I was beginning to feel like an escaped convict. We enterd the lounge and found Daltyboy for the first time after a short night. "Hi" He smiled as we came in.

"What took you?"

"Nothing just some kinky stuff." Said Rocky. He went to sit beside Daltyboy on the divan. The truck driver eyed him swiftly.

"Stay here kid's cause I forgot to buy the milk." The truck driver looked at us all for a moment. "And I mean it, no smart game's with me."

"Hey are we been kiddnapped Mr.?" Asked Veronica. She looked slightly curious. I was beginning to think the same.

"No, and you call me Chuck, uncle Chuck alright."

I suddenly wanted to laugh. Seth was just as bad he kept turning to look the other way. "You want us to call you uncle Chuck?" He asked, with his finger directed to his chest. "Really?"

"Yeah really, and listen Seth I want you to do me one big juicy favor." The truck driver, or uncle Chuck stuck out a finger. "Keep your little smart crack's to yourself, and that mean's you clam up untill I speak to you. Savvy?"

Seth shrugged his shoulder's, a faint smile attacking his mouth. "Yeah uncle Chuck. Savvy." HE put up his hand in a freindly way.

The minuet uncle Chuck had turned his back and gone through the door.

Rocky kicked up a big bralwl. "Now – quick now." He yelled.

"Now what?" Asked Veronica.

"Go lock the door's now, quick cause we don't want uncle Chuck to get back in do we?" Rocky was jumping around like a monky. I suddenly realized that he was right. No we didn't want uncle Chuck to get back in. I ran to the door helping Veronica as she struggled to turn the tiny key in the lock. When it was locked. The both us fell to our knee's as we struggled to slide to the goldish, rusty bolt.

"Great – now that is hunky dory." Yelled Rocky. "Terific, just beautiful. Real cool."

"Hey listen were not gonna be that beautiful, if Uncle Chuck win's the war." Said Seth. "He'll do us to a pulp."

I was'nt so keen on those word's comming from Seth because I knew only too well that he could do better than that. Daltyboy was the only one who had'nt said a word, but when I looked at him he smiled at me and shrugged his shoulder's. "I guess we all have to keep out the big bad WOLF." He said wryly. "Cause I guess everybody has to face it sometime."

I did'nt know quite what he meant, but then I was beginning to feel a little bit like little red rideing hood this time. All of us stepped back for awhile, just standing stareing at the locked door. Maybe I thought we were all waiting for uncle Chuck to come chargeing through any moment.

Seth was the first one to move. He ambled around the room as if he had lost something.

"What's the matter Seth?" I asked makeing myself the second one to move as I ambled after him.

"Notthing. I'm just thinking on how we got ourselve's into this mess like we did."

I shrugged my shoulder's highly, then studied some of the photograph's on the coffee colored wall's. "Maybe we should quit hanging around this place and fly the coop now."

"Yeah why the hell not, we have'nt any glue on our feet." Seth made his way back to the door's. Rocky stood guarding it like a gurrila with no gun. "Move it Rocky." Seth yelled. "Cause we are getting outta here."

Rocky raised his arm's. "Hey but whadder bout that..."

"What about him." Seth flung him away from the door. Then there was the sound of somebody knocking at the door. The door knob was shakeing like crazy. Uncle Chuck was back.

"Hey kid's open up this door I'm back." All of us remained motionless, silent. My hand was pressed tightly over my mouth.

There came another sound. We all turned around to see Uncle Chuck grinning from behind the lounge window. He was tapping on it lightly and in his hand's were a number of milk carton's. "C'mon kid's." He muffled. "Uncle Chuck's back, so let him in."

I found myself near to screaming as Seth and Rocky fought to open up the door. "C'mon." Seth yelled. "When I say run, run."

The door flew open I grabbed Veronica's hand and we like crazy ran for the doorway. We were about to step through when Seth on top of Rocky sent us crashing to a stop. Uncle Chuck was standing infront of us with a face like a watermelon. "So kid's you like to do a little jogging session in the morning?"

I stepped back stepping on Daltyboy's toe's. Uncle Chuck was pushing us all slowly back into the apartment. On his face there was a grin like a sardonic panther. His eye's held all the malice in the world.

"What did I tell all you kid's to do just now?" Uncle Chuck stepped in slamming the door shut behind him. "Did'nt I tell you to keep your damn tail's quiet?"

I could see that grin on his face had vanished. The dark, deep, expression he now held had us all struck dumb as dead as do-do's.

"Well answer me." He yelled. "What the hell did you have in mind? Wat made you do it?" He plunked Seth wildly across the head. The air eurpting lika fire. Seth yelled out.

"What the hell bug's you. What are you a godamed kiddnapper?"

Uncle Chuck laughed throwing all but one of the carton's to the floor.

"No, but you can call me what the hell yah like." The milk carton was torn apart. I watched stupified as he swiftly poured the content's over Seth's head. He darted over to Rocky emptying the rest over him.

"Call me what you like, a sex maniac, a double crossing sex phoney, a big, lousy boyhood assulter, a boy crazy sex digger, a fantastic boy grabber, anything alright. As long as uncle Chuck come's in along the line."

He threw the carton across the room. I watched as he swung around, locking back the door's.

"What about the police." I yelled. "Their bound to find you our one day.They'll come and find us as well."

"Yeah, you can't keep us here forever." Veronica yelled. "It's kiddapp."

"It ain't and I don't give a hang about you two." Uncle Chuck swung around. "But I know you have your brain's. Your not going anyway."

I ran to the door as he pulled Seth aside. The key had gone.

"Get that Tee-shirt off, that milk was cold and you'll catch your death." His hand shot out to Rocky. "And you. I have enough suplie's to make you both feel happy again."

I looked at Seth's over powerd angry, milk dripping face. The milk had made his hair flattened out across his forehead, like a white painted paint brush. Everything about his was a drip, drenched rain bucket. Uncle Chuck grabbed him and milk drenched Rocky like a panther and dragged them both up the hallway. "Now how about me finding you something nice to put on." He hollowed.

Veronica, Daltyboy and I were about to run after them. When I had different idea's. "Hold on stop. We can get out through the window's."

I ran back toward the window. The one where Uncle Chuck had been grinning through, and struggled to open one of the side window's.

"What about Rocky and Seth?" Veronica half whisperd.

The window's were stuck fast like clay. My head spun. I watched as Daltyboy flung him self up to the top window. It was small. But I was only thinking of our freedom.

"I don't know, we can call the police." My finger's were gripped tightly to my hair.

Daltyboy jumped back down again. "That's great – the window's open but how are we through that." He pointed to the tiny gap above that was only enough to let a bird to stick his head through.

"What are we going to do." Veronica screeched. "It's like were inside a casket with the lid banged in."

There was a noise behind us Uncle Chuck had kicked one of the milk carton's aside. "Oh what a pity." He anounced. "What a big clumsy pity. You failed to open the window's and you were all caught red handed by big fat, loveable uncle Chuck." He ambled over toward us. Face like a volcanoe as he slammed shut the window. Then he pounced on Daltyboy like a tiger. He was trying to get of his tee-shirt and jean's. Daltyboy struggled for a while. He was overpowerd. Then Veronica suddenly picked up something. She brought it down heavly like an ax onto uncle Chuck's head.

There was a loud groan from him as he slumped back on to the divan. He was still groaning when Seth and Rocky came flying in. Daltyboy got up. We stood watching as uncle Chuck moved trying to sit up. Then we all ran to the door's.

I'm pretty sure he would'nt forget. Ever. Nither I'm sure would we. Finding the key in his pocket. We unlocked the door. We were free. I hugged Veronica, and I could'nt believe what she had done. What had happened after we had hitch hiked that lift. The truck driver was'nt an oridinary truck driver. He was just another Uncle Chuck I was sure.

As we walked slowly down the street. The sun shone high in the sky like a piece of shinning gold surrouned by a brilliant drape of turquise ribbon. Everything was peaceful no doubt about it. Except Veronica who was still shakeing over her active experience. Rocky I guess was still pretty surprized at her sudden lifesaver. His arm around her shoulder and the smother of kiss's could only bring her back to herself.

Daltyboy who I guessed must be the same, was not the same. Whatever had occured to him in that unforgettable truck driver's pad. He soon got over it. I was thinking this when I let go of Seth's hand. It was with the cool air of summer wind blowing through my hair that I ran like a butterfly down the street. In no time my other butterfly's were following me. Seth, Veronica, Rocky, Daltyboy and I had our wing's so we could fly. I felt as if I had just been carrying a huge backbag. But now the weight has gone and I am free. They are free.

"Hey C'mon let's get organized." I said.

"Yeah and in the middle of San Deigo too." Rocky laughed.

"We can just walk." Seth said. "Anywhere's in the world."

The city air vibrated with music. It was another one of those moon lit night's. Voice's, guitar's, drum's and the sound of dancing feet. Funky town was back in bussiness. Out in the crowd there were kid's of every size, color, height and personality. Seth, Veronica, Daltyboy, Rocky and I were among them.

This was another disco club. Club 45 zero and it was just like any other disco club. From Los Angle's to San Deigo.

The red light's flashed with sempiternal vigor, the beating rhythum of the complicated record's swirled out their music of top ten album's. Kid's chanted as they whirled their hip's, failed their arm's, stepped and turned to the rhytum of the sound of rollicking drum's. The room was hot. The atmostphere good. Like cricket's they hopped from one place to another. The desire to get down. To stay with it. To be a part of what's going on at the disco club of 45 zero San Deigo.

I found my heart alive with a rhytum of it's own. My arm's tingled with an exhilarating new excitement. All I could feel was Seth's arm's around me. All I could hear was the sound of music, music, music.

My whole body now tingled. I could feel Seth's body jerking, vibrateing with sudden, uncontrollable excitement. Jermaine Jackson bowled out his word's over the record. "Close my eye's and I see your face at night toss and turn fall to sleep holding my pillow tight.... all this time I think of you, your with me no matter what I do...... I am feeling what I can't explaine, any question's and their just the same...... let's get serious.... let's get serious... let's get serious and fall in love."

Seth was bowling with the word's as though he knew them by heart. So was I. We danced like mad.. getting serious all the time. Everybody got serious for awhile. They danced with their eye's stareing into each other their arm's tightly locked around crazy partner's, just like we were, Seth and I. We danced with the music dominateing our ear's. I saw Rocky and Veronica really throwing themselve's about. Everything about the atmosphere was good and hot and different. Daltyboy was haveing a good time in the sack with this other guy, kid's around them made them have the aspect of naturebilaty. I put my arm's again around Seth's neck and he tightened his grip around me.

The red light's flashed and six guy's were haveing the time of their life's as they all came hip-swaggering toward us. They all talked loudly, cracking an unstopping string of obscene joke's. Then one of them, the one with long black hair, and a bright yellow headband tied neatly across his forehead started to actively josh Seth around. "Hey, pretty guy, you don't belong here do you?"

Seth looked up, quit dancing and so did I. These guy's were tall. I could tell by the way some crowd's started to back away that they meant trouble too. Seth shrugged his shoulder's. "So, what if I don't?"

There was a brief silence. The black haired guy folded his arm's. "Your pretty chick don't belong hear either."

I looked around at the other's and they just looked back. Then I saw that one of them was colored. He was the biggest and his eye's looked the meanest.

"Hey what are you the manager or something?"

"No, and what are you doing in our club your face don't suite it."

"Maybe your face don't suite it either." Seth looked around. The blackhaired guy raised his fist. "Hey I sure hope that was'nt meant to be a funny, cause if it was you and your darling chick deserve a free lesson." There was a sardonic laugh from the colored guy and I felt my arm summarly been pinned back. The black haired guy held me as though he owned me. I yelled out. "What are you the king? Get your godemed hand's of me now and leave us alone."

"Ha ha ha." He laughed worse than a hyenia. Then Seth exploded like a tiger. "You heard what she said, you lousy bunch of sweathog's. Get your hand's of her and get outta our life's."

That did it. The colored guy stepped forward, pulling out a glinting blade. I screamed loudly. Seth did'nt move, but he just stood there a sharpened sword penitrateing his eye's. "Yeah, so what are you planning to do with that? Cut me to death?"

"Shut your lousy face you fuck breeded son of a bitch." The black haired guy let go of me. They began to suround Seth like a pack of ravenous blood hound's. All the music was still yelling. My heart pounded with death. I felt like pukeing. Then somebody shouted, and it was the manager. He came over in his small form, his grey eye's glareing.

"Okay kid's, hold up what's stalling the harmoney now? What is it the maffia?" Somebody from behind, jabbed me in the back. I turned around to see the gang departing as quick as they had come.

The manager stared at Seth. "What's the storey back here?"

"Notthing, it was notthing okay."

"Well it better be notthing okay, or other wise you and your freind don't come back in here – stand?"

"Hey wait a moment, it was'nt us who started it." My voice was drowned in the music. The manager glanced at his wrist watch, looked around severly for a moment and then ambled back to his box by the D.J.

Seth summarely threw up his finger's. The music blared out and all around the kid's began to stroll back onto the dance floor, dancing slowly at first then energeticly as the music changed tempo. I figured to myself that there had to be an inoncence in it somewhere. I did'nt feel like dancing anymore, niether did Seth so we both went over by the bar and tried to get off with a free drink. "They were just a couple of hard talking nut's." The music had Seth's voice sounding drowning flat. I put my elbow on the bar top and tried to hear him more lucid.

"And what if we are here, their here and it's only a disco."

"Yeah, and nobody not even you two, get away with haveing a free drink." The bartender was looking at us curouisly. "If you can't pay for it, then the law's the law and you don't get anything alright, so move it and let the other's spend around their dime's." His huge bald head flashing in the red light's had the aspect of a red popical. Seth and I moved away, feeling pretty hot. We made our way carefully through the crowd's of swinging kid's and headed finally to the door's.

The cool dark air had me in a trance for a moment. It brushed the glow from my cheek's, my arm's and my neck. Seth was already beginning to amble down the far from familular sidewalk. He started to come back when I awoke, then called out to him. "We have to wait for the other's don't we?"

"Yeah, and that's gonna be around another hour ain't it?"

I shrugged my shoulder's. "Okay I'll go find them and tell them were waiting." Seth shook his dark head, underneath the bright moonlight.

"No, wait those guy's may still be in there, anyway's I'm perpared to hit the sack right here."

My eyebrow's raised. Seth is the one who untimately make's the discison's about our gang, about where we go, about what we do, about where we sleep, and right now I was figuring that he'd gone a little to far, in what he decided was a good night's sleep.

"Maybe we ought both to go in then?" A noisy gang of kid's burst themselve's out through the door way. There was about five voice's singing some crazy lyric's. Rocky, Veronica and Daltyboy were no where to be seen. Seth was just about to agree with me, when they came out. That is Veronica and Rocky. There was no sign of Daltyboy. Patiently we stood around on the sidewalk. Then he came out with another guy. He did'nt see us, but this other guy and him prolonged to kiss each other's and whisper into each other's ear's as though it was the only thing in the world they could do. "Hey Daltyboy C'mon we have to get on now." It was Seth who spoke, he went up behind them quietly, spying on what two guy's could possibly find so erotic, in each other's.

"Okay hang on there.... I'm ... Comming now." Daltyboy was beaming with something powerful. The other guy kissed him on the mouth. Then he departed like somebodie's who's just won a thousand dollar's from the jackpot.

Daltyboy swung around still smiling and waved to us. "Hi, I'm sorry about that, but I guess I just can't quit it."

Seth laughed. "C'mon quit what huh? It's your life you live it." He went up to him, putting an arm around his shoulder. "But right now we need to find somekind of shelter for the night, right?"

Daltyboy nodded his head. "Right."

The street was real empty as the five of us ambled down it. Veronica and I walked together gazeing up everynow and again at the full, round, yellow moon. The sign post around the corner said lower Schatzberg avenue. We ambled down it feeling lighthead and free.

I did'nt really consider that the car behind us was infact follwing us. It was a blue mercead's, the silent type and there was about four figure's hunched up inside. It was following us, and I knew because it was sliding right up along us now.

"Hey maybe it's just a couple of dude's looking for some fun." Seth turned to look at the automobile. Then we prolonged to walk.

"They don't look like a couple of dude's to me." Rocky's voice sounded rather thin. "They look like a couple of plain clothed detective's."

"Let's just keep on walking." Said Veronica. Her voice kind of wavery.

"Um, yes let's do." I guess my voice was sounding the same. We walked on all pretending not to notice this creeping monster. Then we all suddenly jumped aside, as the mercead's screeched to a stop right beside us and a man sprang out clutching a card in his hand. "Okay all of you stop right there. Which one of you guy's go's by the name Rocky Fillpino?" By the time any of us could answere three more men got out, surround us, then layed us all up against a wall.

"C'mon we've been hired to find a runaway kid. One of them is you." The man with the card glanced at it then at Rocky. "It's you ain't it, you fit this discription here perfectly." Rocky nodded his head.

"Yeah that's my name, but that don't mean I'm going with you."

"You are comming with us, and that mean's alot." The man flipped his finger's to the men. They pounced on Rocky like a pack of wolf's half draggin him and half carrying him to the mercead's.

"Hey back off! I'm not going with you alright."

"Leave him go." Veronica yelled. "He's not going back home you hear."

She ran after them as they pushed Rocky in the back seat, slamming the door's shut.

Seth, Daltyboy and I were trying to get past this other man. Then he backed away, running back to the mercead's and jumping in. The mercede's sped away like a thunderbird in the night. "Hey come back here." Yelled Seth. "Come back here."

We were all left yelling a string of abuse to the dark empty street.

Our best buddy Rocky had just been dragged of by a couple of plain clothed men. They were detective's I guessed but I could'nt be sure.

"Is it positive that they were detective's? I mean they could be anybody and we don't even know who."

"Who else can they be?" Veronica was almost in tear's. "They have to be a gang of detective's if they can just throw Rocky into... their cage....and drive him... away." I placed my arm's around her shoulder's.

"Don't worry Veronica he's the strong type, he'll escape in no time." "

From that tight bunch, your kidding." Seth screeched. "They'll most probably kill him if he doe's."

That did it Veronica summarly burst into a bucket full of tear's. She looked at Seth wildly. "That.. was'nt a.. good.. thing to.. say, Seth, it's like.. Rocky.. will get..

killed." She turned away and started to walk down the street. I ran after her.

"Hey where you going I thought we were going to find some shelter together." Seth yelled he ran after us.

"We are, but not if your going to be so damn happy." I yelled. "Our best freind has jusd disapeared and all you can do is make crack's."

Seth laughed and Daltyboy came up behind us. "Hey what's matter with Veronica? She don't look right."

"Yeah and neither is Olivia. She expect's us to cry just because out best buddy has flown the coop."

"Well maybe we ought to." Daltyboy shrugged his shoulder's.

"Why'nt you just grow up, and anyway's what good is that gonna do huh? You explain it to me." Seth pushed him of the side walk. "We have to hit the sack. So c'mon on."

I was still holding on to Veronica as we walked down the dark vacant street. It occured to me that if she could Veronica would do just the same as Rocky. Fly the coop. Her face was streaming with tear's. But in the end she wiped them away when I told her that her masscara was makeing her face look a mess. "Don't worry." I said. "Rocky will be as right as rain once he escape's."

Seth behind us was pointing to something as he yelled. "Hey everybody how about takeing a short cut to the parking lot, it's up behind that little ally up there and I'm feeling tierd."

"Hey, no not in the parking lot." Daltyboy shook his head wildly. "You want us all to be pulp by the morning? Those car's are gonna roll down right over us as though were rug's."

"Nobodie's in them dumbhunk."

"Yeah you wait for tommorrow we would'nt even have enough time to open our eye's before those engine's start roaring."

Seth was just about to throw a real fit when my voice sounded in agreement. "He's right Seth, and beside's sleeping in a parking lot is one of the worst method's I've heard off for getting a good night's sleep." We continued to walk down the street and Seth's temper was boiling at the seam's. It was about another half hour after roaming around various street's that Daltyboy signalled and told us to stop. "Hey over here kid's." He pointed an open doorway of a garage. "It look's real smart don't you think? It'll keep us all shelterd for the night too."

I nodded my head. "Yes, it look's real cozy." I looked at Veronica. She nodded her head. "It's okay."

"Seth?"

"What the hell are we standing here for playing twenty question's" He Yelled. "Let's get moveing." He charged back up the side walk and made his way up the small path to the garage. We all shrugged our shoulder's then followed him.

From outside the inside of the garage looked like a beautiful, cozy, lamplighted room. It was because when we stepped into it the atmosphere was wonderful. "It's so warm in here." I smiled. "We'll all be sleeping like a row of log's." The small oil lamp that was resting neatly on what looked like a rusty little table gave us all the feeling of home.

"Yeah well, then let's calm up and hit the sack." Seth got hold of some moth-eaten comfortor's and handed them around to us.

"But don't you think we ogta.."

"Now what Daltyboy?" Seth flung a look at him. "Your the one who found it so c'mon let's be happy and grab some sleep."

My eye's were drifting just a little curouisly around the place. They rested sumarrly on a small flight of step's leading to another doorway. I was figuring that this doorway leaded to the kitchen of the house. There was a tremendous noise behind us. I turned around to see Seth wrestling like crazy with the garage door. "The damn thing's stuck I knew it."

"Then why make it as though it was'nt." I said. "Beside's we don't actually want to suffercate in here do we?"

"No I guess not."

A while later we were all huddled cosyly inside of our comfortor's.

Veronica though as tired as she maybe refused to lay down and instead with the comfortor tightly wrapped around her sat up stareing out in to the black of the night, for as long as I can remember before I suddenly fell asleep.

We were awoken sometime around dawn by the sound of a passing automobil together with the sound of Veronica's impateint voice as she struggled to wake us up. I sat up to see her pulling of her comfortor then standing up. "Goodbye everybody I'm going home now." My eye's were skeptical. "Anyway's my parent's will be wanting to know where I am and I don't want them to worry." She made her way over us to ward the doorway.

"Veronica come back here, what are you doing your crazy were mile's from home and it'll take all week to get home." I tried to stand up but all my strength had gone from lastnight's disco.

"Let her go." Said Seth without opening his eye's. "It's most probably lover boy Rocky that she's after, and beside's where is she going?"

"Home and I know I'm doing the right thing." Said Veronica. Her hair was in tangle's and she brushed her finger's through it. "So goodbye everybody."

"Goodbye." We all chorused. Knowing that our freind Veronica was'nt going anywhere's paticular on a morning like this when were in the middle of nowhere.

I must have fell back asleep, because when I awoke the sun was really shinning and everything around the garage looked icy cold. Veronica was back in her comfortor. Her face looked haggerd but she still would'nt sleep. From nearby there came the happy sound of playing children. My heart did a sudden somersuauilt. Where exactly where we? We we'nt in an apartment. Then my sense's came back to me. We were in somebodie's garage and we had just spent the night there successfully without any interuption's. I reached out my hand to shake Seth awake and he in turn reached out his hand to shake Daltyboy awake. The place was full of moan's and groan's for a while as we all stretched ourselve's out and stood up to greet the morning sun.

"Boy, some sleep I had last night." Yawned Seth. "It was worse than haveing to sleep on top of a rail way track."

"Yeah me too." Daltyboy arched his back, then slowly rubbed it. "It feel's like somebodie's just stuck a great big stick into my back."

I was almost laughing at them as I stood up. I did'nt feel any better though. Infact I just felt as though I'd just spent the night sleeping on top of a pea. Rather like the princess and the pea I guess.

There came the sound's of a child's voice. It was comming from behind the door at the top of the step's and it looked as though we were about to have a vistor. "Hey Monica you wait there, and I'll go get the ball okay?" The door swung open, a little colored boy jumped out and as he saw us his eye's were suddenly as big as his head. "Hey ma come quick," He yelled. "Cause there's somebodie's in our garage."

Before we had time to do anything, a tall colored woman came out followed by a little colored girl, followed by a macho type colored man. "Why hi there." He said. "What are you all just passing by or what?"

The colored woman was smiling. "Why Frank I think they just need something to eat don't you think?"

"Yeah bring them on in and maybe we can get to know them a little."

My heart was pounding inside of me something a little like a tornadoe.

I looked at Seth and he raised his eyebrow's shrugging his shoulder's. The colored woman was beckoning to us ontop of the step's. "C'mon inside kid's and let's see what I can make for your breakfast."

"Wow is she kind." Seth nodded his head. "Yeah C'mon kid's cause I sure am hungrey."

We all followed him as he mounted the small flight of step's. Daltyboy was yawning like crazy, Veronica and I were just doing the same.

It was warm and bright inside of the kitchen. Bright yellow wall's a blue sparkling floor and a big pink draped window. "Go on kid's." The colored woman smiled. "Go sit yourselve's around the table and your meal will be ready in no time."

We all went to sit around a large wooden table with a white washed top. I was feeling pretty odd. But I was also feeling more than hungrey. There was a clatter of pan's from the pantry and the colored woman came back out still smiling. "Ya'll live around this side or what?"

"No, we've just been travelling." Said Seth. He smiled up at her. "And er we'll be on our way now."

"Then wahat part's do you come from then huh?" The colored man was sitting up at the top of the table reading a paper, and when he talked he looked at us all smiling. "You do belong some place don't you?" Seth nodded his head. "Yeah we'er from Los Angle's."

"Well you must have flown here then." The colored man laughed. "Cause that's quite a while from here ain't it?"

We all nodded our head's.

"Ya'll don't mind what yous eat for breakfast do you?" the colored asked as she fryed something in the pan.

"Um, no not really." Seth replyed.

"Oh, well that is good's cause I only got kipper's meself."

A while later we were all tucking into a plateful of kipper's and hot tomatoe's. Four pair's of black dazzling eye's peeked up at us from the side of the table.

The woman clapped her hand's. "C'mon Marvin, Monica it's time ya'll were at school now." There was a clatter of tiny feet as they both ran for the door's.

We ate in silence for a moment.

"You knows you can use the bathroom afterward's kid's." The man said smiling. "It ain't nothing."

"Thankyou." We all chorused.

"Hey how old are you kid's?" The man's voice sounded curious. "You none of yous look more than your teen's to me."

I was thinking these question's were going to get us all no where. It would probably lead to them wanting to know every thing about us. Even about why we upped and ran away.

Seth nodded his head. "Yeah, we'er in our teen's."

"Don't ya'll still go to school?" The woman asked, hand's resting firmly on her hip's. "Or you is just a load of dropout's?" Her laugh made us kind of laugh too.

"No, we still go to school, but..."

"But your just haveing yourself's a nice.. long travelling vatcation." The man said completeteting Seth's sentence.

"Yeah if you like." Seth nodded his head smiling.

The woman poured some more of her jarva in to our cup's. Her eye's twinkling slightly. A moment later we had all finnished. Seth stood up. "Do you think we could all go use the bathroom now?"

"Hey you is the one's who have to think." The man laughed. He pointed his finger to the doorway. "Yeah go on kid's who's stopping you?" Then he stood up suddenly digging his hand into his pocket. "Here take this, you'll be needing it." He handed Daltyboy a five dollar note. "And see if ya'll can get yourselve's home with it too."

Daltyboy examined it for a moment, before giveing it to Seth. "Yeah, thank's really." Seth placed it in the back of his jean's. "Thank's alot we apreaciate it."

Upstair's the place was as bright as it was down stair's. I looked in the mirror at my disheveld self and almost screamed. Infact we all almost screamed when we saw how utterly untidy, and rumpled we looked.

"Hey I look though I've just come out of a laundery machine." Seth was ploughing a pool of water through his hair as he took a comb to it. He brushed it right back, so he ened up looking like a greaser.

"Oh, I look like a scare crow." Veronica stood beside me infront of the mirror really clawing her hair with a comb and then a brush. I was doing the same. Daltyboy shook his wet hair over us like a drenched puppy. "Hey, now I feel better already. and I bet Rocky is gonna be missing this."

I wet the top of my hair with some water before putting it down neatly and parting it down the middle. "I look alright now don't I?" My freind in the mirror, with a clean face and neat tidy hair nodded her head in agreement and then summarly smiled.

"Yeah and so we all look alright now." Seth said. He looked at me in the mirror, smiling and then we all headed back for the stairway.

Down in the kitchen the air tingled with something new. There was still the aroma of kipper's, but something eles I knew was in the air. As we came in the woman who was standing backing the stove smiled at us and then glanced slightly at her husband. He was leaning over reading the paper, as it lay spread out on the table. Looking up he finished putting on his jacket before smiling at us. "Uh, hi there kid's, you all feel fit enough now? Fit enough to take a ride down town with me? Huh. It'll do you all some good to let me take you back to the police station – and then back to Los Angle's."

I suddenly knew what had happened. All of us must have been in the paper's. We were all running like crazy before a word could be said. Veronica and I for some reason ran back up the hallway. Seth and Daltyboy went the other way running back through the door's that lead to the garage. "Thank's for the hospitallty but we gotta go."

I could'nt tell if we were been followed, but I just ran untill we threw open the door and found ourselve's heading back for the side walk. Then Veronica was sent sprawling as she caught her foot on a small red ball. I helped her up like crazy. We ran on collideing with Seth and Daltyboy as they came running from the oposite direction.

Landing on a heap on the grass. We scrambled to our feet. The man was running out after us. Then we knew that he was a cop. He was yelling something and he held a gun in his hand. "Hey where'd you think your going you kid's? All of you come back here."

I guess we were kind of lucky in a way, because if he had'nt guessed what was happening back there when we did, I reckon we'd all now be in the joint. The air was cool, as we sat together on the bleacher. Seth smoothed back his hair over again and I really though he was beginning to dig that style. We were sitting in a park. In the middle of no where and this was just life.

"Hey so where'd we go now?" Seth wiped his hand's down his Tee-shirt. "Are we gonna find somemore shelter?" Daltyboy eyed him curousily. "Not like that one anymore if that's what you mean." Seth slid on to the grass laying down. "Hey I could stay here all day if I liked."

"I knew what I should have done age's ago." Said Veronica. She gazed up at the sky. "I should have gone home."

"Hey, Veronica." Seth sat up suddenly pointing his finger. "Don't start all that again, or it'll be us who's running from you this time. Not you. Anyway's why'nt you just think of something eles instead of your parent's and Rocky. This is your freedom and your not even enjoying it."

I thought to myself their all just talking a load of garbage. "C'mon." I stood up. "Let's go see what's on in the movie house today, it's our freedom, we got monny and so let's go enjoy it."

"Yeah C'mon everybody she's right." Seth dug into the back of his jean's pulling out the five dollar note. He ran up beside me and we held hand's as we made our way out of the park. It was a really cool day, the sun was shinning and I had not a care in the world.

About a thousand automobil's past us by. The street was crowded with morning store goer's and gang's of children as they made their ways idley to school. I was looking into all the store window's. So was Seth when Daltyboy suddenly came up with something. "Hey, what if that cop's still following us, I mean what if he's told some other cop's? A whole load of patrol's could be wating for us in here."

"Hey kid remember your still one of us, and if you got feet you can run like wherre gonna do if we see any cop's?" Seth turned to look at him. "Are you with me?"

"Huh uh, I'm with you right now." Daltyboy ambled up beside us and we all prolonged to walk down the street.

The movie house, when we at last found it, was'nt atucally like the movie house that we all use to go to back in Los Angle's. It was kind of different, but then it had to be the same if it was a movie house. It could have been a little bit smaller, a little bit colder in aspect or just a little bit unfamilular to our eye's. But anyway's it was a movie house and right now everybody was lining up to watch an old showing of the hit movie "Moment by Moment". It was'nt a really big crowd so Seth, Veronica, Daltyboy and I all got in pretty early before the movie even began.

Seth had it clear that he was paying for us all. Then we brought some of that soft pink popcorn and made our way in to the dark screen room. We had the whole back seat to ourelf's. Then a moment later the movie began.

"Hey I've seen this stuff before." Seth whisperd popping a corn into his mouth.

"Mmm, me too, I've seen it though I don't think I watched it all." I whisped back popping another corn into my mouth. We were all pretty engrossed in it for about half an hour when Seth nudged me in the rib's. "Hey Livvy, this is soppy, so let's fly the coop." He got up and threw his empty popcorn packet onto a girl's head. She swung her head around wildly. "Will you just bequite." She whisperd in a loud voice. "Where all trying to watch this movie."

"Well I'm not, I'm getting out of here." Seth whisperd back. "And so you can all just watch it by yourself's."

I was still watching the movie when I suddenly realized with anger that he had really gone. I shook Veronica and Daltyboy and we all made our way out of the dark room to the entrance of the movie house. Seth was waiting for us all when we got out. Veronica yelled out to him. "Seth that was'nt fair – you did'nt like the movie but we did and just because you came out we have to come out too."

Seth laughed at us. "Yeah that's because the movie was real soppy and I don't dig soppy movie's even if my best buddie's do." I stared at him hardly for awhile before I continued to eat my popcorn. "Seth." I said a moment later. "That cop back there did not give us that monney to throw around, and that's what were just doing now, I mean we could have watched that movie. It was beautiful and you just had to spoil it for all of us."

"Oh my darlingg it was beautiful, it was truly beautiful and now I've gone spoilt it." Seth was on his knee's makeing up some kind of romantic act and I knew that if I did'nt love him enough it would truly have been his last romantic act.

Veronica and I were laughing now so was Daltyboy. He was stareing at Seth as though he was a crazy. "Hey now everybody come to think of it he doe's do it all a little bit better than John Travolta, don't he?"

I shrugged my shoulder's, looking at Veronica. Then we both chorused. "Maybe."

"Hey C'mon." Seth stood up. "Root for me huh."

We did root for him finally, before ambling back down the street. We went into a drugstore, buying a packet of ciggerate's to drag while we waited for the disco door's to open.

The music blared out, kid's swarmed in, everything was hot with the sound of drumming drum's. We danced to the music for hour's. Wilder grew the music wilder grew the kid's. Hoter grew the atmosphere, brighter flashed the light's. Seth danced with me like crazy. His arm's coverd over woundingly in a mass of red ring's. Just before the door's had opend he and Daltyboy had been stubbing their arm's with the tip's of their ciggerate's. They had been trying to see who could stand all the pain the longest. I reckon it was to see who out of them both could be named as the strongest, plus the bravest. Though Daltyboy managed about eleven stub's, at least four more than Seth, I still figured that he was the one more closer to tear's when they both finished, finally. But I think it was because they swoped over after awhile, beginning to stub each other's arm's and that's when Seth gave Daltyboy a really long one.

The disc jockey was yelling out over the music, though I'm not sure if it was him or the person who was singing out the record. "C'mon everybody let's hear ya clap your hand's, stamp your feet and come alive with the rhythum of the boogie beat.... clap your hand's... stamp your feet and come, alive, with the rhythum of the boogie wogie beat..."

I clapped my hand's, like Seth was doing only he was clapping his just a little out of time from the rhythum beat I thought. We swung around like lizard's, stamping our feet with the drum's. Seth was throwing back his head, his whole body twisted with the urge to jump up, dancing with his back flat down I reckon he had the knack of dancing just like an islander in the tropical continent, makeing his way swiftly underneath a dancing pole.

We must have been danceing like this for hour's, hour's and hour's. The music never failed to get hotter. The kid's never failed to quit dancing. We just danced all day like our feet were glued to the dance floor. I began to think that Seth had a real reality about the way he danced. Because not once did he change that dance style.

Then it was when I was beginning to think I would drop if I did'nt quit the dance floor soon, that there was a frenized burst of noise, followed by one mad shout. The dance was over and all around everybody went on a crazy rampage. Blade's flashed like lightening underneath the bright red and blue light's. Blood spilled like water as they stabbed at each other's with malice. There were loud pirecing scream's from either boy's or girl's. Poster's were torn of the wall's.

Bottle's and tin's were thrown through the window's. Clothe's were ripped off as kid's tried to strangle each other's with their tee-shirt's or jacket's. Record's went flying. Glass went flying. The light's stopped flashing as somebody finally tore them down, sending the whole room in a agony of murky, pitch blackness. Nobody was nowhere to be seen. All I could see was blackness. All I could hear were scream's, scuffleing, stabbing and plunking. I called to Seth. But the music was loud. I could'nt see, hear or feel him. Nobody was going to quit what they were doing even if they could'nt see to do what they were doing. I clasped my arm's over my head. Bottle's and tin's came flying from nowhere. My ear's went on fire as they whizzed past them at 75 miles an hour. I found myself sinking to the floor, suddenly overcome with exhaust. My eye's were tightly shut only makeing the room grow darker and darker and darker.

Somebody was helping me up. Was it Seth? I opened my eye's, could'nt see a thing. It had to be Seth. I suddenly found myself wishing it was'nt Seth when whoever it was, summarly was blown away from me. I continued slowly standing up. My arm's reached out infront of me as I stepped into the direction of the entrance. Something red splashed over my hand's. I put them to my face and I knew that it was blood. There came a big explosion. I thought myself almost to the doorway. Another explosion with the sound's of fadeing police siren's. Then there was the sound of something rushing, like the sound of a rushing huricane and I was suddenly thrown back by something as powerful as a tornadeo.

I was drowning in something like a splashing waterfall. Kid's came flying from all derection's. Landing on top of me like a ton of crashing brick's. I felt my ear drum's bursting as running ice filled my ear's with something swirling. My breath was failing. I was gasping from either lack of breath, or overpowering coldness. I was feeling a little bit like a disapointed Peter of the dyke, the boy who was susposed to have saved Holland from a dam burst.

Then I realized that the cop's had suddenly turned the hose on us. They could'nt get us out any otherway so instead they had decided to use something more powerful. Maybe though I thought. This was the only way to calm up a crazy mob of hell-raising stabbing kid's. It was working too, because nobody was no longer stabbing with blade's. But instead we were all swiming around like a school of crazy, flying fish.

In about, what seemed like a week the cop's decided to cease all the water. The room was still like a pit, moreover like a swimming pool and all of us teen-ager's were compeltely saturated to the bone's.

"Okay, now everybody. each and every one of you get out. Your all under aresst. You have a right to remain silent. Anything you say now may be brought against you as evidence on the trail."

"Oh, yeah and who say's so." A voice rang out.

"Okay that's number one." Yelled the cop. "And any more of you who dare say another word the same go's for you."

I was trying to see who the cop was because right now his voice was sounding all of pretty famiular. he yelled again, this time louder.

"C'mon now alla you get out." And that's when thing's hit a snag. The whole place was just like a roaring stampeade again as kid's every where ran charageing for the door's. I heard about a dozen shot's ring out, and I was wondering why the cop's were shooting if they could'nt even see what they were shooting at. I felt myself been pushed toward the door's like a jolt from a volcaneo. Everbody was crazy as they fought tooth and nail to get themselve's near the entrance. I found myself doing exactly the same thing because for some paniky reason I just had to get out from this place. It was like we were all scrammbleing from the inside of a building, where a bomb was just about to explode.

Blindly I clawed my way past people untill I finally reached the entrance. I was no longer worrying about Seth and the other's, because at the same time I was thinking that they must be doing now, the same thing that I was doing now. Then I reached the entrance and all I could see was a thousand waiting buzzard's. Cop's were everywhere linning the street's and I was just about to make my escape when somebody grabbed hold of my hair, suddenly pulling me aside. "Hey, don't I know you, ain't I seen your face someplace before?"

I looked up into the face of the colored cop. He was the same one who had took us all in this morning. I nodded my head with a flash of pain travelling sharply through my scalp as the cop kept his hold on my hair. "But I have to go.. now."

"Oh no yous don't cause your comming right along with me."

There was a splatter of feet as kid's ran storming from the building to possible freedom. Sound's of bullet's rang through the air. Cop's charged around knocking kid's to the ground with the butt's of their gun's. I tried to break free from this other cop. But he kept a strong grip on me, dragging me from the building to a large black police van parked along the street.

The whole place was a rageing choacas. Cop's and kid's struggled like crazy sending shower's of ice cold water into the darkening skie's, as they fought to get them into the van's. The cop without mercy pushed me into the van, and slammed back the door's, before locking them. I turned around to see a whole load of drenched dripped boy's sitting, staering with blade's in there hand's. My eye's rounded.

"Hey it's a girl."

I must have been pounding at the door's and yelling for age's before one of them got up and swung me back around. "Hey girl, listen are you gonna clam up cause were all gonna get outta here somehow."

I nodded my head, before they all went crazy trying to kick down the door's. "Hey I've been in here twelve time's and I ain't gonna be in here for another crazy second."

"No, everybody neither am I." They were all yelling as they fought frenzily with blade's to break away the lock. "C'mon everybody let's show's these lousy cop's just what we can do."

I stood there watching, dripping and shivering half with fright half with icness as each of them took it in turn's to throw themselve's at the door's. My teeth natterd. It was useless we would never get out. My finger's wrapped tightly through my hair with nerve's. Then the door's did open, but not from the inside.

There was only a brief flash of the colored cop as he pushed somebody eles into the van. Then all hell broke loose. He did'nt even have a chance. The boy's were all crazy as they scrambled down from the van. They lashed out with their blade's, half trampling him as they charged out for their longed for freedom. I found myself doing notthing but running away from the van. My clothes's were drenched and I was tripping like crazy over the end's of my jean's. Cop's and kid's were still all around but I found myself getting past them all, as easy as pie.

I ran in all direction's untill I caught sight of Seth running down a street. I followed him, yelling out his name as I did. He did'nt stop running so I began to think he was getting death. "Seth wait." I yelled. I finally caught up with him and he turned around.

"Hey, listen I think you've got the wrong guy, okay?"

I was stareing up into the face of this round faced, acne faced boy and I could have died. "Oh, um I'm kind of sorry about that, but I thought..."

"You thought I was somebody eles? Yeah well that's okay cause I don't care about that kind of stuff anyway's." He grinned.

“Mmm, yeah.” I laughed. “And your wearing all the same clothe’s as him too.”

“Yep.. well I’ll be on my way then.”

I watched in a daze as he kind of continued to run down the street. Then I turned back around and did’nt know where in the world to go.

I just wanderd down the sidewalk infront of me. My teeth nattering as though they would do so for the rest of my natural life. I had strange theory boiling at the pit of my stomach that Seth along with Veronica and Daltyboy had been caught out by the cop’s and bundled into one of those black van’s. It did’nt help me to think that they had been so I just tried to forget about it all. I tried to imagine they were with me right now. Though it was impossible with the loud sound’s of police siren’s filling my ear’s. A black automobil screeched around the corner. it’s front light’s glowing in the comming darkness. My heart did a kind of sommersualt, but I just walked on.

No police car’s stood infront of the disco club when I ambled back to it and no cop’s were hanging around with gun’s in their hand’s ready to shoot at the first kid who came out. It was all peaceful and quite. I hung around for awhile not knowing exactly what to do. An elderly couple saunterd past me. Their face’s both written over with fear, sadness and sypathy.

The water trickled down from my hair line to my nose. I wiped it away. I went to stand shiveringly in a nearby koisk box. It was about twenty minute’s later that I heard the sound of running feet. Three figure’s ran by one was limping and I just pushed open the door and stepped out. They were the only people in the street and I called out to them. My thought’s resting on Seth, Veronica and Daltyboy. “Hey you kid’s wait a moment.”

Not much later I was answered by the sound of screaming tyre's. I could hear a voice yelling out to me. "Hey Olivia where you been." It was Seth's. Then there was a dramatic collison. I heard as car door's were flung open, six tall figure's came running from the street on to the sidewalk. They seperated us like a herd of cattle. "Hey now I can't say we ever picked a finer time to come across our old long time disco buddie's. Can you guy's?"

"No man we sure can't."

I gaped at them transfixed. They were the same guy's who were with us in the disco.

"Hey so whadder bout it Doug?"

"Whadder bout what?"

"The cause and time of death. Why'nt you just go finish your work off with that pretty faced guy over there."

My hand suffercated my scream as I pressed it tightly over my mouth. I was thinking of going back in to the koiosk box, but my feet would'nt move.

"Yeah lord hows about just doing that huh." A silver glint flashed into the night. A scuffling sound broke out. Seth and the guy with the blade were fighting like a pair of lashing crocadile's. I screamed for what seemed like hour's before one of them fell tumbling to the ground. There was a frenzied yell then the rest of the gang were running like crazy to the crumpled heap on the sidewalk. I yelled out for Seth, then my heart almost sang with joy as I saw him come running up the street with Veronica and Daltyboy staggering behind. "Quick everybody into the car." I heard him yell. Then I saw as he suddenly stopped and threw up his hand's into the air. They were coverd in blood. The moonlight shone down on them ludidly. "Jesus, no, I've just killed that guy." Seth was hysterical but we all ran for the car, scrambling in like crazy into the seat's.

Seth managed to start up the exillarator. The engine splutterd out. The sound of running feet together with the roar of the engine filled our ear's. The car was just screeching off to go when somebody yelled out. "Hey come back here stop – you lousy low down bloodhound's you just killed our buddie."

"Stop – stop you crazy bastard's." A voice screamed. "Stop cause were gonna lay out your gut's and hang you all – your murder's, your all gonna die."

We did'nt have enough time to shut the door's. They were all hanging on to them like a bunch of savageing monkey's. I screamed out at Seth to drive on faster. He was swerveing franticly as the guy's all tried to jump into the car, trying to knock them off as each of them all clamberd up onto the roof. The door swinging back near me was suddenly, frenzily ripped away as one of them grabbed onto it and was sent flying into the street. He landed like a bullet in a heap of garbage bin's. Veronica was screaming like mad. Her arm's were pressed tightly over her head. "Were gonna crash, were gonna were gonna crash I know it."

Seth screamed out. "Christ....christ... christ I think were all gonna die... I can't control this car ..."

"Help hey help.. everybody.. I'm dieing.." It was Daltyboy. I looked up to the window screen to see a flying body, gripping onto the roof of the car. Seth crazily screeched around another corner. The body stayed where it was, blindingly blocking our street view. Seth was yelling out at the same time as he tried to shake away the frenzied, clawing guy on the front of the car. "Jesus.. I can't see... christ I've gone blind... jesus... jesus.. jesus help me.. I . I can't.."

The car swerverd to one side. To another side. We were rocking around like crazy. I yelled out. "Seth..help were going to crash." My eye's caught sight, blindingly from behind the swinging body, the eldery couple who

I had seen passing me by. I screamed out as the car headed straight for them. Their horrified face's. "Seth look out look out your gonna hit them.. were gonna crash." I franticly reached over for the steering wheel. But was powerfully thrown back as we swerved madly into another direction.

The guy ontop of the window screen was suddenly thrown off. He was sent sommersuaulting into the street, crashing and rolling around like a tennis ball. I screamed again. But we could see again. Seth was franticly pressing down his foot on the pedal. We were getting faster all the time. Veronica was screaming loudly. I turned to see one of the guy's still hanging onto the door. He was trying madly to get in. I tried to push him out. Veronica clung to me tightly. He was suddenly thrown clear as Seth took another sharp bend around a corner. He landed in the doorway of a house I was clinging to my seat as we raced yet again around another corner. If I did'nt I was thinking I'd go flying through the doorway. Seth was getting expert at his driving. We careered around for another five street's, before we all heard the distant sound's of screaming police siren's.

"Hey, c'mon where we headed?" Seth was yelling out again and the car was getting dangerously wonky.

"Just keep on driving... keep on driving the cop's are after us." I swung around to see the flashing light's of a police car. "Seth we have to go faster."

"Yeah I'm trying.. I'm trying, I'm driving this car.. but I can't control it..." Seth almost let go of the steering wheel as we screamingly rounded another corner.

Daltyboy yelled out. "I'm dying god.. I'm dying, stop the car man.. I'm dying man." He was clinging to his seat, eye's closed tightly and his face a deathly white. "Aaahg... starrrp the car.. Seth.. starrrp it... please."

We smashed like crazy through a whitewashed fence as we screeched around another corner. I swung back to see that we had lost the cop's. There was still the sound's of police siren's. We were screaming like a whirlwind into a dark empty ally. Seth was pressing his foot down on the brake's, and then we all skidded to a stop.

None of us could say anything for awhile. We just sat stareing out into the dark empty ally. Seth was sitting with his head bowed down in his hand's. He did'nt move. But he just sat there. I pulled my hand's through my hair trying to blot out from my mind what had just happened. It was one of the craziest moment's in my life that I could obtain. I was'nt thinking or breathing right. I was almost gasping for breath and my heart was pounding away like a steel drum.

I turned around to look at Veronica after awhile. Her clothe's were drenched to the bone and her hair was madly disheveld. Infact we were all drenched to the bone. All of our clothe's stuck to us thinly like glue, and our hair was as wet as the nigaria fall's.

"Oh my head's spinning, and I think I'm gonna puke." Veronica was half way leaning out of the doorway, with her hand's clasped around her head.

Daltyboy opened his eye's. He began to groan suddenly like an old man. "Help... I'm dying.. everybody help me... I'm dying..".

My eye's were resting strangely on Seth. He was summarly awake as he sat up and looked at Daltyboy. "Shaddup, were all dying.. were all gonna die so quit it." He turned his head, looking at me with tired, darkened eye's. "You alright Olivia?"

"Mmm" I shook my head. But I was stareing at Seth in a strange and different manner. He looked different, and he talked different. It was like he had summarly mateured in second's. I felt a kind of icy shiver ran down my spine.

Seth was different he had just changed. He had killed somebody. I put my face into my hand's, something cold hoovering around me.

Something loud and bombarding was screaming through my ear's as I opened my heavey eye's and sat up from my crumpled soggy position. It was the car horn. It was blasting off it's head and Seth was leaning on it as he slept with his arm's thrown around his head. I reached over weakly, and tryed to pull him away. He did'nt move and the screaming continued.

It was early morning, the sun was just about awakeing and I was feeling as dog-tired as a hound. Daltyboy acompanied the horn blare with a severe amount of dying cough's. In no time I was doing exactly the same. I felt as though I would sooner die than choke over my endless cough's. When Seth awoke he was just as bad. I looked at Veronica, her hand was pressed tightly over her mouth, before she half dragged herself out of the car to a nearby garbage bin. An old bum ambled by clucthing a whiskey bottle in one hand. He looked down at Veronica bitterly, disaprovingly as though he's just lost a thousand dollar's worth in gold.

Daltyboy was clucthing his side in agony when I looked back around. He groaned something awful. "I've just been stabbed, hey kid's I'm bleeding." Seth had his head away from the wheel now, the horn quit it's blasting. He stared down at Daltyboy's side. "Hey my god it's true. Daltyboy's bleeding like a water fountain."

I reached over gripping on to the front seat. Daltyboy's whole white tee-shirt was as red as a berry could ever be. He held his hand desperately over a frenzied stab wound. "Oh lord. Daltyboy your gonna be okay."

Veronica stumbled back into the car, her face drained like a sheet. "I've just puked up a mountain and I feel like I could die."

"Yeah well Daltyboy's just been stabbed and I bet he feel's like that too." Anounced Seth severly.

"Oh you creep." Raged Veronica. She struck out at him savagely. "It's all your fault. You got us into this mess, you got Daltyboy stabbed, you got me sick by your crazy driveing, you made us hitch that godamed crazy lift, your the one who draged us into that disco, your the one who got into that fight, you killed that guy, you stole this car and your the one who made us up and run away."

Seth did'nt say anything, he sat stareing out into the front for a moment.

Then he exploded. "Oh yeah, you crazy bitch, you really think so? You really think that I got you into this MESS, then why the hell don't you get your ass outta here?" He swung around like a tiger.

"I think you did Seth cause your a bastard."

"Your not a bastard your a bitch."

"You think you know everything, but you don't."

"Shaddup."

"No, you killed that guy, and you expect us to stay with you, you expect us to do everything YOUR way."

"I'm NOT gonna kill anybody eles, but I will if you don't shaddap."

"See I told you Seth you are a bastard you are a murderer, your a traitor a bloody cold blooded traitor.."

Seth lashed out at her. "I said shaddup you bitch, go find your crazy loverboy Rocky or go to hell."

"You just have no heart."

"Neither do you."

"Your nothing."

"Your nothing."

"Bastard." Veronica spat.

"So god help me but if your heart don't attack you now I WILL."

Veronica clawed at him. "You would'nt DARE."

"Shaddup, shaddup both of you." I yelled. I suddenly pulled Veronica aside. She stumbled from the car yelling, crazily and ran up the street staggering in her high heel's.

"Veronica." I yelled. I climbed out the car. Seth grabbed my arm.

"Olivia leave her." He screamed. "Let her go."

"No." I broke away, running up the street after Veronica. She ran on and on without stopping. "Veronica." I screamed. Then she suddenly stopped, doubling over as she puked all over the place. "Veronica." I caught hold of her as the roar of an engine attacked my ear's.

Seth yelled out. The car was comming straight toward us. I pulled Veronica aside like crazy. She was struggling and trying to break away. Seth suddenly skidded to a stop. The bonnet was inche's away from us. I pulled the hair from my eye's and put my arm's around Veronica, as she prolonged to puke up the street. I was almost gapeing at Seth as I lead her back into the car. He was just sitting with his eye's fixed before him and his hand's in his lap.

Veronica did'nt say another word. Her face was drained, and her hair was madly disheveled.

I looked at Seth as he started up the car again. "You almost killed us Seth. Why?"

"He almost killed me too." Daltyboy was still groaning.

"It was like you really wanted to, you know?"

Seth was'nt answereing. He contrated on the road ahead of him. We drove out from the ally, leaving it behind as we turned the corner and found ourselve's in a main street. I kept my arm around Veronica. The side of her face swelled up, blueishly from where Seth had struck out at her. My mind was a million mile's away. I was suddenly wishing on being back home with my mother, my home and my house. With all famiular surounding's, my little red dairy, my brother and his beloved honda motorcycle. I was just wishing that I could be home. To drink a refreshing mug of hot chocolate. To have a cold refreshing shower. To go back to high school and be back in my class. Change my clothe's, brush my hair, clean my teeth, do everything that I could forever do at home, and I knew right now that this was the only thing that I craved for.

The street was half vacent as we cruised along it. Nobody had awoken yet. But the sun was shinning like a diamond in the sky. I looked across at Daltyboy and he was shakeing wildly, like a leaf. His whole body was in sudden concluvsion's as he bent his head onto the dashboard and coughed as though his bone's would break. "Seth don't you think we oughta take him to a hospital, he don't look too good?"

"No.. I'm.. not going.. into... any.. old.. hospital." Daltyboy had sat back up now. "I was'nt.. born in.. one.. and I'm not.. gonna.. go in.. one now."

Seth looked at him crictially. "You'd better cause you......" He was cut of sharply by a whole mound of coughing. Daltyboy was shakeing again and he looked awful sick. He stopped. Then started again as Seth reached out to touch his forehead. "Hell man, this guy's sweating like a steam boiler, he don't feel hot but he is."

I reached over, touching Daltyboy's forehead with my finger's. "Dalty boy your real sick, your bleeding and so we'll have to get you into a hospital now, no matter what."

"Hell no. I don't wanna go into no hospital." Daltyboy spluterd, as he coughed again. His arm's were clasped tightly around his shoulder's and he was shivering more than ever.

"Well you are Daltyboy, now." Seth suddenly pressed down his foot on the peddle. We were zooming down the street in no time like crazy.

"Seth we don't even know where the hospital is." I was summarly aware. "Which hospital are we going to?"

"I don't know but were headed someplace, it's either that or Daltyboy is gonna find himself someplace far."

"But where Seth? Where?"

"I don't know. But it may turn out to be something like paridise."

"No Seth where? Which hospital?"

"I don't know I told you, but wherever it is I know we have to get there fast." Seth pressed his foot down harder. The car raderr was reading 75 mile's an hour. It suddenly shot up to 80. We were tearing down the street like crazy. "Seth." I yelled. "Do you want the cop's to be after us, your driveing to fast."

"No, I don't, I have to drive fast if were gonna find that hospital, and I don't want any ambulance's chaseing us eiether."

By the time we had coverd about sixty street's, sixty roadsign's, sixty mile's and asked about a thousand passersby where for the love of Mike the hospital was. It was about 2.30 in the afternoon and Daltyboy was looking pretty much like a cemertery. He was shivering, coughing like crazy by the time we finally got him addmitted to a hospital. The nurse took one look at him, one look at us. Then she had him eliminated into a sickbay and us put aside for a hot drink and a change of clothe's. It was something that I'd been longing for age's. They were warm, cozy but crisp and I reckon I looked kind of different as well as tideir in the grey and white zipped up sweatshirt and blue levi's. Infact we all looked so cleaner that we did'nt seem to mind if the clothe's did come from people who were now in the morgtary.

Seth was still marverling over his new clothe's as we all sat in the waiting room, flicking through Life magazine's and reading the no smokeing, health poster's on the wall's. He was beginning to act like a baby who's just received a new toy. "Hey Olivia don't you think theas levi's were just meant for me?"

I was beginning to get interested in one of the Life mag's.

"I look like them don't you think so?"

I was interested in one of the Life mag's when I finally shrugged my shoulder's, and looked up. "Yes Seth okay, they were meant for you, they are you if that will satisfy you." I continued to read the magazine. Veronica was doing the same. Her hair neatly tied back in a ponytail, and the skirt and greenish top fitting her a real treat. She still was'nt talking so I decided not to disturb her.

We had been sitting there for hour's when a nurse finally walked by and Seth sprang to tackle her. "Hey nurse, scuse me but do you know anything about Daltyboy yet?"

"No sorry I'm very busy right now." The nurse hurried past him in her sqeeky white sneeker's.

Seth threw his arm's up. "Christ you don't even open your mouth before these little white creature's dig up dirt over you and tell them that their busy and oh you'd better go find somebody eles to throw your trouble's at." Seth sat down and almost broke the chair as he did. This all went on for what seemed like week's.

Altogether about four nurse's walked by, each time Seth asked for Daltyboy each time they shook their head's and told him they were busy. Then about an hour later nurse second to the last came along. Seth sprang up and tackled her. "Hey listen nurse, do you know anything about a guy named Daltyboy?" The nurse frowned, but she stopped. "Daltyboy? No, but maybe if he was a horse I might do." She ambled by without waiting for an answer.

"No damn it, it is not okay." Seth almost yelled. He was in a real fit now. He slammed down the Life mag he had been reading and stormed out of the waiting room, chargeing back up the corrider to god only know's where. I had a feeling to go after him. But then I changed my mind when I saw yet another nurse comming up from the opossitt direction. I summarly ran up to her. "Um excuse me, do you know anything about Daltyboy?"

"Daltyboy?" For a while the nurse looked puzzled. "Oh is he maybe the one up in ward six. The one who has phemonia and a possible stab wound?"

I nodded my head thinking the worse. "Is he okay. Is he gonna die?"

"Well I don't know about dieing from a stab wound but I heard of many case's where people die from phemonia." She rested her hand's heavly on her hip's. "Chance's are though he may pull through."

"Yes, well is it okay if we go in and see him now." I was hopeing she would just ask no question's and let us all go along. But she did. "Do you all belong together? I mean are you all his brother's or sister's? Are you family?

"Freind's." I pleaded. "But we have to get in."

"What's the patient's real name please?"

"Um, Dalton Verrazano."

The nurse frowned slightly, pericing her lip's then beckond. "Okay then follow me you may as well all come in." She looked around for a moment.

"How many are you?"

"Three." I glanced around seeing Seth ambling back up the corrider.

Veronica put away her life magazine and we all of us followed the nurse.

Daltyboy was laying back, with his face as white as the pillow when we came in. He looked weak as he sat up and stuck out his thumb. "Don't worry kid's I'll make nice with this hospital if it does me good." He smiled. Then almost choked as he broke into a spasm of severe coughing. Seth went to sit in the bedside chair. "Hey man, you don't look so cozy on the eye as I was expecting you to. You look sick."

"He is sick." I said as I sat in the opossite bedside chair. "But I know he's into getting better too."

"And that's just chinch." Daltyboy was seeming alright again. He tried to sit up. "Cause all I have to do it find my clothe's and fly the coop."

"Maybe, Daltyboy but you have to get better with some help." It was Veronica who had suddenly spoke. She was sitting on the end of Daltyboy's bed, compeltely egoring Seth. "And so I guess you'll need to stay in this place."

"Hey man what's the heat? I'm razor blade sharp, and still all you kid's think I'm real for been ill." Daltyboy blinked his eye's as though annoyed. He looked at Seth. Then smiled slyly. "Hey your not really thinking on leaving me here are you? Your not gonna leave me behind?"

"I guess so." Seth played with his finger's. "But bare up on getting well again and I know you will."

"Aw jeeze, no I wanna get outta this place now." Daltyboy blinked his eye's again. I was thinking he would now if he could. But he broke into another round of coughing and that seemed to settle it. "I guess I can hang in for another day or so, but that's all."

"Yeah, were sure gonna miss you too." Seth looked up.

"You see if you don't."

"And we'll be going to the disco tonight again." I said. "But we shan't actually be running away from you. We'll stick by as close as we can."

Daltyboy smiled. "Good. You do that." He summarly stuck out his thumb again. Then suddenly coughed, before finally sinking back into the pillow and closeing his eye's.

Of course we all hated to do that. But I guess we just had to. It was something that cut us all to the heart. Haveing to leave our best buddy Daltyboy behind, in a strange hospital, with strange people that we did'nt even know and strange surrounding's that he did'nt even like.

The nurse had handed me a red polythene bag with all our clothe's in. They had been all throughly washed and neatly ironed, and then she had anounced that we could come back anytime tomorrow and visit Daltyboy. I was thinking when we ambled out of the hospital, that our buddy was really bad now. But then I was thinking that tommorrow our buddy would be really good too. I was thinking that he would get better before we even had enough time to make our way back to his bedside, or even back to the hospital.

We got back in to the car. Seth managed to drive it back onto the road.

The sky was pretty dark, with a faint glow that the moon was about to make it's apearance. "Where shall we head?" I asked. I was thinking right now that we were heading no where in paticular. "Somewhere's."

Seth shrugged his shoulder's and almost collided with an on comming pick up truck. "So how about going to a drive in."

"A drive in? but how do we find one?" I was sounding surprised.

"I guess he just want's us to look for one." Decided Veronica, airly.

Veronica was sitting in the back. I was guessing too that she still could'nt abide with Seth.

"So, I guess we'll just look for one." I decided.

We did evenually get to find one. It was pretty crowded and the film that was on was only a disney produced cartoon. Seht was almost asleep when he got out suddenly. "Hey I think I'll tear off these resistration number's okay, cause I know those guy's are gonna be searching like mad for this car."

"Okay." I agreed. "But don't you think we oughta dump it instead."

"No I don't think so." Seth was already around the back tearing off the first resistration number. Then he went around to tear of the front one. "It's gonna be okay, cause look, there's alotta brown mustang's about here." He pointed to about ten brown mustang's all sitting in a row, before heading over to one of the drive in garbage bin's and dumping the crumped up number's in.

Then he got back into the car.

"I still think you oughta dump it." Said Veronica.

Seth said... "Okay we will dump it, we'll dump it just as soon as we get outta the disco." He turned around to look at Veronica. His eye's gazing slightly. "Okay?"

Veronica nodded her head. "Okay."

Seth turned around to look at me. "Okay?"

I nodded my head. "Okay."

The disco that we finally managed to find was'nt actually a crowded one. But then it was'nt exactly a big one either. Infact it was one of the smallest disco's that I've ever been in. It was the same atmosphere though. With red and blue flashing light's, swirling, blareing music, swinging kid's, hot, sweltering air and the sound of a mettlesome voice as the D.J. yelled out over the record's.

Seth and I were dancing together, when he suddenly stopped and called out to Veronica. "Hey, Veronica don't you think you oughta stick by us tonight?"

Veronica was danceing on her own in the crowd. She quit dancing. Then nodded her head. "Okay." She came over and then we were all dancing together. I guess it was safer because those guy's I was thinking could still be hanging around the place.

We danced madly for about an hour and then we decided to come out a little bit earlier than before. We ambled up the street just takeing our time and gazing up at the dark moonlit sky. Seth had decided that we should all sleep in the car tonight. It was stationed some way away in the parking lot. Just around the corner actually, and so we were headed that way now.

We were just turning the corner when Seth suddenly stopped and pointed to the parking lot. "Hey, give a look at that."

Veronica and I looked up. There were about twenty or more black leather jacketed boy's all on scrambler's and all stationed surrounding our brown mustang. They looked about the same age as us. But I thought they all looked like a couple of hell's Angele's, too. They all seemed to be waiting for something.

Then one of them arubtly did a high up on his bike and left the pack roaring away into our direction.

"Hey C'mon." said Seth. "I think we oughta get outta here."

We were just about to, when the rest of the roaring bike's filled the street.

Thousand's of yellow light's were falahing into our eye's through out the dark street. Then everything went silent as they roared past us, away up the street.

"Hurray." Cried Veronica. "I knew it was going to happen they went straight past us and we did'nt even have to run."

"Yeah and I thought it was trouble for us." Seth clapped his hand's like Veronica was doing. "Anywhey's we've still got our old mustang."

I rooted with them nodding my head. "Yeah so let's go get into our old brown mustang." We were all just about heading up to the parking lot. A roaring sound of yelling engine's burst through our ear's. We all turned around to see the sudden purpose. They were all comming back, tyer's and all. "Quick." I yelled. "Run."

Crazily we ran into the direction of the parking lot. Then Seth doubled back. "Over here – it's better." He skidded around a corner just as the bike's were almost ontop of us. I was running like a bullet. So was Veronica. She clung franticly on to Seth. Yelling all the time. "Help, help. we have to run. Seth hurry – hurry. Their gonna catch us."

We stopped arubtly to find ourself's in a dusty derlict building. I was panting something awful so was Seth. He crouched down beside an old knocked out window beckoning to us to do the same. "Sussh, don't say a word or we die."

Outside there was breathing, brushing leather, twisting glove's against handle's and the put-put sound of stalling engine's. Somebody was talking in a low demanding voice. It got louder. Then fierice. "We got eye's. We know your in that building so get out."

Seth threw his hand over Veronica's mouth. She looked near to hysteric's.

I crouched down further into the strewn mass of garbage. Clamping down my eye's shut.

"I said come out. We don't dig kid's who take our car's for joyride's." There was the heavy sound of footstep's. "Infact we usally punish kid's who do thing's like that."

Seth stood up pulling us with him to another corner. Then Veronica suddenly tripped over a can. It was sent bouncing onto a wall. The noise was deafening. The footstep's were nearer. "Where gonna kill that nice little buddiy of your's, cause we know which hospital he's in and we know you took him there."

Seth suddenly yelled out. "How? You don't know anything about him. You lousy hog's."

"You'll see cause were gonna split him."

I had a sudden vison of poor Daltyboy laying in his sick bed. "You can't it's crazy. He's got notthing to do with you."

"He has a lot. Kid's who steal car's usaully do." The rear of motor bike's filled our ear's. There was a final yell from the youth. "And when we finnish him. Lookout you lousy, lowdown fuck-head's cause you killed our buddy and your gonna pay for it." Running footstep's roaring engine's and yelling voice's was all that we could here as the hell's Angele's mob roared angerly away into the distance.

It was a while before any of us could manage to say anything. My heart must have been at least pounding ten time's it's normal rate, because all I could really hear was that. Seth stared out at his hand's. He was sweating something awful. It was like he had a fever. He brushed them over his face. "Jesus god it was all my fault. I should have killed them all. I should have killed them." He yelled. He stood up suddenly running out from the building. "Yeah, you lousy godamed, square headed bastard's I killed your buddy. But hell I did'nt mean to I swear. I did'nt mean to kill him."

Seth was acting as though he was going to run off down the street. Then he stopped and suddenly he was back in the building. "C'mon everbody we have to go tell Daltyboy we have to warn him. We have to get outta here and back up the hostpital."

"Yeah let's go." Yelled Veronica. "We have to go help him." She got up and ran for the doorway. I picked myself up my heart still pounding and followed her. Seth was already half way down the street by the time we got out. "Seth hold on a moment." I yelled. "We don't even know which way the hospital is."

"We do." He swung around. "Cause we can still make it in that mustang if we try."

We were all running like crazy before we skidded to a stop outside the parking lot. The mustang was still there. Seth ran to it. Then he suddenly threw up his arm's like mad. "Hell, those lousy punk's have gone and smashed up the oil tank. They've managed to slash up the tyer's too.

That doe's it everybody. We walk." The bull in Seth was beginning to paw the ground. I hastily managed to grab hold of the red bag, through a splinnterd smashed window before running after him. Veronica followed and we all three of us ambled down the street, in the dead of night by ourself's. "How long do you reckon this is going to take us?" I asked. The path ahead of us right now was'nt looking too clear.

"No question's asked, just keep walking. Were in a hurry."

Veronica nodded her head in agreement. "Yes and we have to get to the hospital tonight to tell Daltyboy."

“Okay no need to salt the wound.” I clucthed the bag tighter underneath my arm’s. “Because I reckon we are going to get there somehow.”

We had been walking for what seemed like hour’s in an ice cool dessert when Seth summarly stopped. He sat down on the side of the sidewalk, putting his head into his hand’s. “Heck, how the hell do we get ourselve’s outta this cobweb?”

I sat down beside him. “I don’t know but I know I’m tuckerd out that’s all.” I was thinking that what I could do now was to hit the sack. Seth looked up into the sky. “Okay so let’s not cry for the moon. No hard feeling’s Daltyboy, but I don’t think were gonna make it tonight.”

“Can’t we just hitch another lift?” Veronica asked. She was sitting down on the other side of Seth, slowly takeing off her stiloute’s and rubbing her feet. “We’ll get there awful quick you know.”

“Yeah I know, but I don’t think so.” Seth lowered his eye’s. He ran his finger’s through his hair. “Cause we don’t wanna end back at uncle Chuck’s house now do we?” He lay back on the sidewalk, arm’s tucked underneath his head.

I suddenly thought about Daltyboy and the hell’s Angle’s gang.” “Oh for christ sake you two your talking loco. Daltyboy’s going to be killed if we don’t hurry and get there now.” I stood up, starting to make my way down the street and just simply forgetting about my tiredness. “Seth are you comming with me or not?”

Seth rested his elbow on the sidewalk as he rolled over. “What differnce is that gonna make? I ask you now. I mean those guy’s have most probably already cut up Daltyboy, jumped back on there motorbike’s and gone to japan.” He rolled back over and lay back down.

I looked deasperately over to Veronica. She shrugged her shoulder's and shook her head. "He's right Olivia I mean we can't even find the building, and what good is it gonna do if we walk? Huh?" She turned her head away and prolonged to rub at her feet.

I summarly turned and wallked down the street. I was only thinking of Daltyboy and I was going to save him, with or without Veronica or Seth.

Seth did'nt do anything forawhile. Then I heard footstep's as he came running up behind me. "Hey Livvy where you going huh?"

"Don't ask dumb question's Seth, you know damn well where I'm going." Seth laughed. "To save the queen huh?"

"No, not actually, but I'm going to save Daltyboy."

"My god really?" Seth put his arm around me. "Well maybe you can give me some line on how we get there? Tonight."

"Well I guess I'm figureing I don't know. But I know we have to save Daltyboy tonight."

"So do I, hell but we can't find him so we may as well hit the sack." Seth threw his arm's up. "It's crazy, c'mon we can go in this park here."

I looked around, seeing a dark eerie gate, then a grasy park. Veronica came up behind us in her shoeless feet. "Hey what's going on here I thought we were stopping the night?"

"We are." Seth pulled open one of the creeking iron gate's. "In here."

"In there?"

"Yeah in there. What's the matter you scared of spook?"

Veronica threw back her head. "Huh, no not in this world anyway's."

Seth ambled in. He pointed to a distant bleacher. "Guess that'll make nice."

We followed in. I was still on to thinking of Daltyboy. But I was soon thinking back on how very tired I was right now. "Hey don't you think were all going to get a little blinded by the morning."

"Now what kind of loco are you talking about." Seth had already layed up for the night. He was rolled out on the grass. "Are you really been into superstious?"

"I guess so." My pillow was about to be the clothe's filled red bag. Veronica was trying to make nice with the bleacher. She was planning on makening her stiloute's as her pillow. Seth yawned tuckerd, before placeing a tuckerd arm around me. He gazed up at the shinning moon then closed his eye's. "Terific dream's Olivia. Night – Veronica."

I gazed weakly at the shining moon. "Good – night Seth. Good – night Veronica?" Veronica I was figureing had at last made nice with the bleacher. She yawned. "Good – night Seth. Good – night Olivia." Then she rolled over and all was quite. I looked up at the moon for a moment longer, without seeing any form of a cheese. Then I summarly fell asleep.

Lawnmower's, playing children and the sound's of passing automobil's all made sure that Seth Veronica and I did'nt exactly have the perfect summer-time lay in. I awoke with all those sound's attacking my ear's. Even the sun managed to skin awake my eye's before I had the teenist chance to open them. I finally did, only to find that I did'nt have a dime in the world to know where we were. My mind was blank. "Hey Seth do you have any idea to where we are?"

Seth was just about as bewilderd as I was. He shrugged his shoulder's looking up at the sky. "Yeah I reckon we've found ourselve's right beneath the sun."

Veronica yawned tiredly. Trying to put back on her stiloute's. Then she looked up. "Were in the park, yeah I remember last night we stopped here."

"I hope it's not central park." Seth stood up. He ambled around the park like an unolied tin man. Then sat down beside Veronica. Pulling his finger's through his untidy crop of dark hair, and yawning.

"We have to go save Daltyboy, now I remember." He said.

"I get to thinking that were already too late." I picked myself off the grass and decided that the red bag I had used for my pillow was'nt so bad after all. "Mother of god I wished we had made it last night. It was impossible, but we could have found the hospital."

"So let's go there's no time to hang in." Seth made his way to the gate's.

We followed and were on the street again. Someway along a tribe of long haired beetnik's passed us by. One was carrying a radio and that's how we got the time. It was almost 9.45. As we passed there were a few "Hi's" in exchange. We ambled out into another street, before we realized what was standing out a head of us. "Jesus christ, it's the hospital." Yelled Seth. It was too. Standing right infront of us, and the letter's stood out boldly underneath the sun. (SAN DEIGO FIRST MEMORIAL HOSPITAL).

"My god I think we've gone crazy." Seth was already makeing his way like a bullet toward it. Veronica and I followed. We almost got knocked over in our sudden haste by an on comming volvswagon as we crossed the street. "Wow." Cried Veronica. She clung onto me as we scuttled past it. "I thought we had, had it."

I was far too shocked about the hospital to care about the collison. Seth had already got in through the entrance and was ambling up the corrider before we finally caught up with him. "Do you know which corrider has ward six?" I gasped, tuckerd.

A passing nurse turned around surprized at us as we raced by. I guess she was thinking that we all looked like a couple of clothe-worned hobos. "No I don't but I guess we can ask somebody." Seth almost collided with another nurse. "Hey, um sorry. Do you know where ward six is please."

The nurse looked at us as though we'd just been thrown from a spaceship. "Hav'nt you kid's been here before?" She inspected us acusingly.

"Yeah, but we've lost our mind's, so we don't remember which corrider our buddy was put in." Seth sounded impateint. He looked at the nurse anxoiusly.

"Just go along this corrider, turn left and you ought to be outside ward six – okay." The nurse smiled.

"Yeah thank's." Seth raced on, summoning us to follow. We ambled down the corrider passing by the waiting room. Then we were outside ward six. The door was hanging wide open. My heart did a sommersuault. We went in to find notthing but an open window and a pile of sheet's neatly folded up ontop of a flat, bald mattress. Seth threw up his arm's. He voiced my thought's with anger. "Christ it's happened they've killed him, they've killed our buddy Daltyboy. Christ if I could get my hand's on them I'd break them."

Veronica was gasping with a drained face. "Daltyboy – no I don't beleive it. Daltyboy no not Daltyboy it can't be true it is'nt true."

"What shall we do." I felt my heart dying with greive. "We'll have to tell somebody – quick."

All of us made our way out of the room mawkishly. A passing nurse stopped to question us, her eye brow's raised in astonisment. "Are all of you feeling alright? You look quiet sick to me."

“We are sick.” Seth utterd with a deadpan expression. “Our best freind has just been killed by a couple of punk’s.”

“Now then kid’s I reckon that this is’nt the kind of place to be playing around with game’s, I think you should all leave this hospital now.”

“Don’t you belive us?” I gasped. “It’s true they said they were going to do it and they did.”

The nurse suddenly went over to talk with another nurse. Then she ambled back. Her expression was no longer surprized. “Oh I understand now your looking for the boy who once occupied ward six? Dalton Verrazano is it?”

We all nodded our head’s. My heart was suddenly half dead, half alive. “Well he’s been transfered to another ward.” Seth suddenly awoke up in to a gasp. “He what? He’s been transferd to another..”

“Yes and if you go up to the second floor you’ll find him, he’s in ward number eleven so it should be easy to find.”

Seth could have hugged her. So could have Veronica and I. Daltyboy was’nt dead. He had’nt been killed by those leather-jacketed punk’s. He was alive, and I just could’nt believe it.

“Oh my god thank’s.” Said Seth. He was almost laughing, and so was Veronica and I. Maybe I was thinking, as we all ambled toward the lift that the nurse was thinking that we were all a cople of crazy screwball’s. She just stood watching us for a moment as though we were just that.

Veronica I reckon had a strange phobia about travelling in lift’s, because when we reached it she suddenly stopped dead with her hand across her mouth. “Hey listen you guy’s, I – I think I’ll just take up the step’s instead because I hate going in lift’s.”

Seth threw up his arm's. But he smiled. "Okay we'll all use the stair way, cause we don't wanna lose each other do we?"

"No we don't." I agreed. So we all made our way to the large flight of step's. As we mounted them I had the weird feeling that I, was actually mounting the step's to a large, invisable areoplane.

A couple of nurse passed us by when we landed on the second floor. We turned a corner. We turned another corner. We turned another corner and then we found ward eleven. Seth pushed open the door, and it was a sight that I'm sure we would never forget for the rest of our live's. Because there was Daltyboy, sitting propped up with a large white pillow behind him, a bunch of grape's in one hand and a comic book in the other. He looked up when we came in and summarly smiled. "Wow hi there kid's." Seth stared at him as though he'd just seen a ghost. Veronica and I were just about doing the same. It did'nt look at though any of us could beleive that he was – alive, actually sitting up in bed, alive. Seth ran over to him. He was touching him all over like he could'nt belive he was there. "Hey, Daltyboy are you really with us? Are you really sitting there in flesh and blood, your not a spook are you?"

Daltyboy was stareing at him in surprize. Now it was his turn to gag.

"Hey hold on, waite a moment, Seth I know that you love me but you don't actually need to make it that lucid." He glanced across at us before throwing us the bunch of grape's. "Hey take those, cause their your breakfast."

"Daltyboy you were going to be killed." I finally managed to say. Daltyboy scoffed the two remaining grape's, he had snipped off from the bunch. "Talk english – as much as it hurt's you."

"No, Daltyboy it was true, you were going to be killed, they said they were gonna come and do it." Veronica said as she hungerly tucked into her share of grape's.

Daltyboy studied us all acusingly for a moment. He laughed. "Then how come I'm not up there yet?" He pointed skyward. "And anyway's who go's by the name they?"

Seth was about to eat another grape. He stopped half way. "The gang don't you remember, the one's whome we stole that mustang from?"

Daltyboy broke into a severe bout of coughing. Then he nodded his head. "Man, yeah now I remember. Well, what's the matter don't they really find me attactive enough?"

All of us laughed as he made a small pretence of grooming down his hair. I was figureing that Daltyboy just was'nt going to take our storey as a serious one. Seth shrugged his shoulder's. "Well maybe they did but you have to get outta here, cause those guy's meant it."

"What? I'm allowed to come out, ray." Daltyboy began to root. Then he stared at Seth. "Are you actually into takeing me home?"

"Yeah because those guy's could hit this place any second."

Daltyboy lept out from his bed. "That's great. And all I need to do is to find my clothe's." He ambled over to a white cabinate, pulling out a tray with his jean's and tee-shirt all smartly washed and ironed.

"Don't worry kid's." He said. "They are my clothe's."

"But how do you get out of here, with all those nurse's?" Veronica asked.

"I just, you know stay right behind ya'll and eveything'l run smooth."

"Gee, I'm hungery. Whered you get those grape's Daltyboy?"

"Not from my parent's if that's what your thinking." Daltyboy laughed. "Well, this blonde nurse gave them to me. she just said hey kid your great and you deserve some candy."

"They did'nt actually taste like candy." I said remembering the way grape's do taste.

Daltyboy shrugged. "I reckon I don't dig candy eiether."

Seth stood up and looked through the window. "Think you can make it down there Dalty?"

Daltyboy had just about finnished struggling into his jean's. I thought he looked pretty much like a skeleton without his tee-shirt on. He pulled it on then went to stand by the window. "Your kidding I'd be dead before I touched ground."

Seth laughed. "You really thought I meant it huh?"

"No, cause I really think you love me Seth." Daltyboy put his arm around him. "And your really gonna get me outta here too, ain't you?"

Seth nodded his head. "Yeah, cause I don't tell lie's when it come's to keeping promise's Daltyboy and that's the truth."

We made it around the first corner. Then thing's began to get different. Nurse's began to look at us rather curosily and the docter's were worse. Daltyboy kept well behind us. Then he suddenly doubled back.

"Hey you guy's – that one know's me. Quick." A tall grey haired doctor, carrying a medical card under his arm was heading our way. He looked as though he had already seen Daltyboy. But we did'nt give him a chance to say a word. We were all back down the corrider in no time. Daltyboy was the fastest. He skidded around a corner and almost bumped into a nurse. It was like this for about ten minute's before we finally managed to stay clear from any docter. All of us headed for the stairway.

Then we were back on floor number one. Seth lead the way. I was beginning to think that we would never get out. Daltyboy crouched well behind us. He's a little bit smaller than Seth so he was well coverd. Veronica and I though we did all our best to hide him. We both managed to look pretty much like ourselve's. Then I saw her. It was the same nurse who we'd met the previous day. The one who had told us about ward six and she was headed straight in our direction. "Quick, everybody split." I said. I did'nt actually mean split, but I meant run. Seth skidded to a stop. All of us collided into him. The nurse had seen us. She was getting faster. We dragged Daltyboy back around the corner.

"Hey C'mon I want out."

"Sussh." Seth peeked back around. "Jesus that nurse is still on us." We all ran like crazy down the corrider. I could still hear the sound of her sneaker's going squeak, squeak squeak, and I reckon that they were getting faster all the time. We got faster too. But we had to hold up when two nurse's suddenly came from nowhere. They ambled by Seth stareing at us curroisly. We kept our eye's glued to the floor. Daltyboy almost dropped one of the comic's that he had skyjacked from his ward. They were stuffed underneath his tee-shirt. A doctor ambled by. My heart was pounding. But he suddenly turned back, calling out. "Hey, don't I know you, pateint? Ward eleven Verrazano?"

Daltyboy almost jumped out of his skin. Seth backed him up. "No um sorry, guess you go the wrong one. This is pateint number six."

The doctor glanced at his medical card and we vamoosed. Daltyboy sprang around the corner. He suddenly broke into another of his coughing fit's. We somehow managed to help him along the corrider. But in the end he just had to stop. That's when I heard the squeaking again. Daltyboy was sounding close to dying.

We had to pull him along again before he finnally quit coughing. "Hey, now which way do we go guy's?" He gasped.

"This way." Seth pointed out toward a flight of step's. We crazily ran toward them.

"Why can't we use the lift?"

"Cause I don't like them." Veronica gasped. "They make me puke."

Even though we were now headed down the step's. I could still percieve those dreaded sneaker's. I was thinking they would alway's be in my dream's. Squeak, squeak, squeak. Or was I only imagineing they were.

At the bottom of the step's we all collided to a stop. A group of nurse's were standing discussing something. Seth decided to shrugg them off. "C'mon you lot, just act cool and they'll never hear a pin drop." All of us managed to act cool, stay cool. The nurse's did'nt even look ourway. A couple of wheel chaired patient's, a couple of nurse's and a couple more unknown doctor's. Then we were out through the back way of the hospital, like Seth had suggested.

Daltyboy let out a sudden, dramatic "Yippee." And pranced around like a monkey. "Wuh hoo, everybody, I thanks ya'll for getting me outta that straight- jacket. Man I could'nt even breath in that thing, let alone live."

Seth slapped him lightly on the back. "Yeah well, now your free, now I'm free and now their free." He thumbed over to Veronica and I. "So Daltyboy what doe's that make us all huh?"

Daltyboy grinned. "Man it make's us all free." He glanced up suddenly to look at the sun. Then he summarly lowerd his head, kissing Seth on the cheek. "And that's for you buddy, cause your the one who really got me outta that slum." He smiled, as he pulled out a windfall of comic's from under his tee-shirt. "And these are for you girl's a whole lotta funny's to read."

He planted a comic in my hand and then he gave one to Veronica. "Okay, now fan's so where are we gonna enjoy our new found freedom."

Seth shrugged his shoulder's. "Well how about down freedom road?"

"No, I got it, how about takeing a trip in our old mustang huh? We can cruse around a little you know?" Daltyboy sounded exited.

"Only we have'nt got it anymore." I quitely anounced.

"What our pretty littl mustang has really flown the coop?" Daltyboy summarly frowned. He gazed at us all enquiringly. "What made it go?"

"Those guy's, you know those punk's, well they done it over sometime last night." Veronica was flicking through one of the comic's. When she summarly laughed. "Hey, you know something I really dig these kind of comic's, cause Charile Brown is one of my greatest superstar's, thank's alot Daltyboy."

Daltyboy shrugged and smiled again, "Yeah, and so, I used to read all about him when I was around six or seven."

We all laughed, before finally ambling away from the hospital building to our new found freedom, and this time Daltyboy was with us.

Well like we all figured we'd do. We did. We had freedom, inside disco's, on the street's and in the park's. By the way we also managed to hitch another lift to Santa Barber. that's where we had our real freedom. Several week's went by, and we spent most of our time ringing up all the fancy hotel's. Though most of them were booked, I reckon we were just enjoying all the kick's, that we had from doing it.

Also we found another disco club. It was on the north side of Sanderson square and it was pretty big compared to other club's. Disco club 17 was something different. Seth, Veronica, Daltyboy and I all went in one night for only one thing. That's to dance away the night.

"C'mon everybody let's have some fun." The powerful voice of a D.J. filled the hughe, over crowded disco club hall. "Whoever you are, wherever you're from and whatever you are were gonna have a good time tonight."

The crowd responded by leaping into action. Dancing and yelling their approval. "This is no sit-on-your-hand's music." Screamed the D.J. "It's get-up- and-dance-and-think-and-feel music. so C'mon ya'll this is the kind of music you can all rock to – let's see ya hop to the beat." Everybody hopped to the beat. "Let's see ya rock to the rhyum." Everybody rocked to the rhthum. "And now I want ya'll to come – alive." The D.J. continued, giving away his strong Californian accent as we all came alive with the music. Seth and I were really rocking around. It was one of the best disco's I think that I've ever been too. I guess it was all the tremendous engery and enthusiasm of the kid's that got it really going. Almost every culture was there. There were. Orient's, Asian's, colored's, canadian's and red indian's all simply haveing a mighty good time. There were even a few beatnik's, gay's and hetersexual's all haveing a good time to the music. I was thinking that Daltyboy could'nt actually be dancing like crazy because of his freshly sticthed up side. It was'nt actually giving any trouble. But just before we all went in Daltyboy had made it clear that he was'nt going to get the whole wound come undone again. So I reckon he was right now haveing some fun. But that he also had his hand pressed tightly over that sticth. Well anyways we danced around untill two in the morning.

When we came out the moon was still gleaming. It was a pretty cool and peacful night and the only problem we had now, was to where we were going to book up for the rest of the morning. Seth suggested the youth hostel down the street. So that's exactly where we hit the sack.

By going to the arcade for at least ten time's a day and with Seth been the one who won all the dime's, we managed to save up quite a lot of dollar's. It cost only five cent to go on every machine. So by the time we had competled them all anybody can imagine just how crazy Seth got when he found out how swell-lucky he was.

We also got into some pretty fancy restaurant's. Only to buy thing's like tootie frutie's, hot fudge sundae's and tunna-melt sandwhiches's. But I guess we all had enough in just been there. It was about a week after our first disco in Santa Barbabar. Seth had just orderd another round of tootie frutie's and life was just great. I sat opposite Veronica and Daltyboy sat opposite Seth. It was one of those resturant's in which we got to meet almost everybody, flimstar's like Slim Mcagee, Toddy Montgomery and Stacy Vanherpen. Popstar's like Felix Gambina, Russian Teenie and The New York Highlight's, Dean Splendor and The Summertime Hassle's. I reckon we were kind of lucky to meet them all. Flesh and blood and in a restaurant too. The waiter who had paid some attention to Seth's request was all and all takeing a little too much time on comming back. Finally though he did. "That'll be 75 cent's each please." Seth handed him the bill and then:

"Oh my gadmother of Jefferson Davis it's our old buddy – it's Rocky."

"My gad so it is." I yelled. "It's Rocky."

"Rocky Fillopino where in the wide world have you been." Veronica was up on her feet before he even got the chance to say anything. The both of them just gazed at each other. Rocky with a big wide grin on his face and Veronica with her mouth half hanging open.

"Rocky I can't beleive that it's you." Daltyboy marvelled. I marvelled. We all marvelled. Rocky was just a fantastic guy. He had changed like lightening over the week's. He had grown taller. Seth stood up and like crazy he came him a great big bear-hug. "Man, Rocky where in heaven have you been?"

"I done know but I been somewhere's guy's, cause like hell I've been a missing you." His voice had dramaticly got stronger. It had matured. There was notthing more than smooth talk now, all his rough crack's had suddenly vanished. Veronica rushed over, giving him another dramatic, identical bear-hug. "Rocky you don't know how MUCH I've been missing you." His comical, floppy waiter's hat went sommersuaulting to the floor. He swung her around and gave her a fire-cracking kiss on the lip's. Mother of Jehova all his mass of dark, thick, once beautiful glossy hair had been totally shaved off. It was so closely cropped, that for a single moment I thought he had gone bald. "Rocky what in the world has become of your hair?"

Rocky kissed Veronica again, before he touched his new hairstyle. "Hey, well don't you love it. Make's me look kinda sexy huh?"

"Hey, you look as though you've just had a fight with one of them lawn mower's." Daltyboy yelped. "Man I think you've gone bald."

I don't know what everybody in the resturant were thinking of us all right now. But actually I reckon they all thought we had gone nut's. I mean, it was just like Rocky, (been a waiter and which has really truly surprized, because I was thinking he just did'nt suite it) had recieved a gigantic tip from somebody whome he thought would be the least generous. Right now we were meeting up with a buddy whom we all thought had disapeared from the earth.

Seth and Rocky triumphingly did the slap-five. "Wow is it good to see you?" Seth sang.

"Yep, and is it good to see you."

"Where you been man?"

"Home and around."

"And did you enjoy your long long vatcaition?"

Rocky's eyebrow's did a high up. "Whadder you kidding, I had myself outta that place before them adult's even had the chance to say: Rocky pack your bag's and be on your way. You don't wanna settle down like a nice, smart, decent kid, so pack everything you own including your drug's and get out."

"Hey, they really meant that?"

"They really meant that."

"Whadder you gonna do now huh?"

"Act sensible. I got myself a real smart, reliable pad. With everything from the floorboard's to the ceiling, and I got myself a real smart room mate." Rocky stcracted his head. "No I forget he left a couple of week's back, but that don't matter cause now I got myself another tribe of room mate's, and beleive me, your gonna be living in that pad by tonight."

"Hey, is that the truth?"

"And notthing but the truth."

Seth did a dramatic sommersualt into the air. "Whey, hey jesus man did you here that everybody we got ourself's a great, new shelter for the night."

I began to root like crazy and Veronica and Daltyboy both helped me to shower out our approval. "Hey, Rocky that is just terrific." Daltyboy was acting as though he'd just got it all made. Infact all of us were acting as though we had just got it all made. It was like something big and wonderful had just flown around us all and rescued us from a large, black murkey pit.

"Rocky, I think you've just about come, saved our live's." I contined to root, and so did the rest of us until I thought we might never quit.

It had been such a mindblowing surprize that in the end we just simply forgot about our second round of tootie fruitie's. Rocky had it all in his mind when he suddenly showed us around to the back room of the resturant. "Hey, here you are guy's and now you can just about get your teeth into anything."

"Wow is this some kithen." Veronica anounced. "It look's more like a laundry room."

I looked around at the dull stained wall's, steamed up window pane's and the large stack of dishe's and decided that this in everyway was a kitcthen and not a laundary house.

Rocky was busy. He made sure that neither of us all would ever get hungrey again. "Hey, you guy's, you like real, trendy eat's like Lasagna and hot fudge sundae's?"

"We love them." Seth was slowly studieing the place. He looked as though he was about to redecorate the whole area.

"Man I've been eating so many of those hot fudge sundae's that I don't get to feel the cool anymore." Daltyboy croaked.

"I really dig Lasagna though, it's swell." My mind was telling my stomach that right now all I ever needed now was a decent meal. Something that I had'nt had since I left home.

Seth suddenly asked: "Hey, Rocky how much bread do you get for doing all this stuff then?"

Rockey held up all his finger's. Then smiled. "Fourty live saveing dollar's a week, aint that neat?"

"Yeah, man that's neat. That's real neat." Seth gave him the thumb's up sign. "A dollar here – and a dollar there." Then he smiled and Rocky continued to prepare for us his really special return treat.

Well anyway's we finally got to see Rocky's new dwelling. It was on the east side of the resturant, and it was just a few block's away from the disco, someway a way from Sanderson square. The whole block of about sixty to seventy apartment's stood solitarely on a little stretch of land which had been nicknamed the "vacant lot", because of it's sudden romoteness away from the rest of the street's. But here on Fitzgerld street it was like a hollywood to us.

Rocky's pad turned out to be notthing more than three seperate room's. But we all thought it was swell. The floorboard's were completely carpetless. While the only peice of visable furniture to be seen was the bed that Rocky now occupied and the single bed that his pad mate use to occupie. Over the wall's there was a tatty, asortment of poster's. They were either curling up at the corner's or simply dropping off the wall's. The ceiling was okay. With no sign's of any secret hole's. There were drape's on the window's, and all this together with the sight of Rocky's tremendous luggage, had us thinking that home sweet home once again was just around the corner.

Everything went smooth on the first day. We just made ourselve's happy by smokeing some more of Rocky's old marijuana. He gave us all large quantie's, while we listened to the radio. We sat on the floor, crossed-legged most of the time's just dreaming that we had been sitting there for hour's instead of minute's.

Rocky played some of his best-loved record's on a pretty worn out recordplayer. It had been something that he just some how managed to drag all the way from L.A.

Rocky had also managed to get us all in with out the landlord finding out a thing. He continued to do his job as been a waiter, because how in the world was he going to pay the rent for the apartment? and at time's it had been said that the landlord good get pretty nasty if he did'nt recieve the weekly pay of ten dollar's.

All went well. All was bliss. It was raining out side and I could here the sound of pitter-pat's against the darkening window as the rain attacked it. Seth and Rocky were haveing a game of backgammon, while Daltyboy was sitting half shivering with a grey comfortor wrapped close around him. Lately he had been coughing bad. But Rocky with his smart idea's had given him several dose's of the marijuana, and it had some how helped to ease them a little. I was sitting crossed-legged on top of one of the cot pillow's, my back resting wearily on one of the wall's and my eye's firmly trying to read another chapter of Ed McBaine's breath taking book "Long time no see". It was a peaceful commuian, together with an aproaching dusk, and I looked mildly across at Veronica as she sat cross-legged like me, with her back to the wall and her eyes firmly resting on one of her fravoit Charlie Brown comic's.

It was about a minute later that she came over to sit next to me. I was still into my chapter when I felt her slightly nudge me. It was as though she was trying to tell me something so I quit reading and glanced up at her. "Anything the matter Veronica?"

"No, not really, I was just thinking about my mother, she'll still be wondering where in the world I am I guess."

I nodded my head, understanding. "Yes, mine too. Infact all of our's I reckon." Another wave of darkness stole across the room. I peeked back into my book and began to read another breathtakeing page all over again.

In a while later the same nudge in my rib's was repeated. Veronica was looking at me strongly this time. Her eye's dark with a growing weirdness around them.

"Olivia, have you any experince to what it feel's like?" Her voice sounded even weirder. Almost as though she was somebody eles.

"What, feel's like what?" I asked slowly as I closed my book.

"You know, how doe's it feel to be...?" She parted a strand of lose hair behind her ear. "How doe's it feel to be...?" Another wave of darkness brushed the room. I was beginning to think that Veronica was not her usall self. "How doe's it feel to be..? I don't know." I said as I hopelessly shrugged my shoulder's.

"To be... do you know... what... it feel's like... Olivia?"

"Why, don't you get to the point Veronica, because I have'nt a dime to what your talking about."

Veronica almost subsided as she let out a long, tuckerd breath. "Well... my mother know's what it.... feel's... like.. it.. it was a long time ago." She played slowly with her finger's. Then she looked up at me. Her eye's heavy with a trace of diffulty hovering inside them. "It was bad at first because she had several.. misscaraige's, but then she had my sister. Wilma was okay she did'nt.. die like the other's.. and neither did.. Veron.. he lived.. too." Veronica lowered her head and continued slowly to play with her finger's. "And then I came along I was the last one... the youngest and.. I lived.. too."

I still could'nt find head or tale to what Veronica was talking about. I listened to her with growing puzzlement, with all the while the room getting pretty dark.

"But.. you see.. Wilma.. and Veron are... not.. my.. real brother and sister. Well.. they are... my.. brother.. and sister.. naturally. But.. you.. see."

Veronica looked up at me darkly. "Soon.. after they.. were born.. my mother.. got a divorce, she got married soon again, and then I was born. My father is really good... to us all, but he.. already know's you see.. that Wilma and Veron.. are not his.. real.. children and every time.. my mother look's.. into.. their eye's.... she.. told.. me that.. she can.. still see their father in them... their real.. father."

"Yes, but what has all this got to do with what you've just asked me?" My mind was roaming round and round to try and find what exactly Veronica was getting at. Veronica parted another strand of hair behind her ear.

She looked at me for a while. Then she got up and ambled away briskly, into the direction of the bathroom. A moment later she was back. I could tell that she had just been puking because behind the hazy darkness of the room. I could detect how very pale her face was. She sat back down again. Her hair slightly dissaryed.

"Veronica?" I asked. "Are you really feeling alright?" I was thinking that she was only feeling a little nostalgic. Then she looked up at me her face hollow and drawn in the darkness. "No, Olivia I am not feeling alright because because I'm pregnant."

"Your? My god I don't beleive it." My heart did a sudden sommersualt. I glanced round the room to see if the other's had heard. But they had'nt Seth and Rocky were still playing backgammon. Daltyboy was still sitting huddled in his comfortor, without the slightest notion that he had heard. I looked back at Veronica. "And you mean to tell me that this is what you've been trying to tell me all a long?" Veronica nodded her head.

"Mmmm, uh huh." She bit her lip, and slowly placed her hair behind her ear's.

I stared at her anxiously. "Are you going to tell the rest?"

She shrugged her shoulder's slowly. "Shall I?"

"Who's baby is it do you know?"

"My god. It's Rocky's of course." Her voice had suddenly changed. She brushed a hand over her face. "And I guess I have to tell him."

"Okay." I nodded my head slowly, and helped her to stand up. We ambled out into the center of the room. Nobody had regonized us yet, not even Daltyboy. I went over to where Seth and Rocky were playing backgammon on a small wooden table. Even then they did'nt look up. "Everybody. Veronica has got something to say to you." My voice was pretty echoey in the silent room. Seth looked up, and then Rocky.

"Like what huh? She want's to go home again?"

Rocky gazed at Veronica. "Hey, C'mon you've only been here two day's." For a moment they just gazed at each other through the darkness. Then Veronica stepped foreward. "Rocky... I'm.. I'm pregnant."

The room was awake as Rocky suddenly laughed. "Hey, Veronica c'mon your only haveing me on are'nt you? Cause I don't believe you right now."

"Well you'd better believe me." Veronica's voice was stern.

"Why huh?"

"Because it's your baby."

Rocky suddenly stood up. "Hey, no. my god anything but that." His hand's flew to his head. "Hey now, c'mon Veronica your lieing are'nt you?"

Veronica shook her head. "No Rocky it's true – I'm pregant and your going to be a father."

He ran up to her suddenly, grabbing her by the wrist. "Hey, now C'mon Veronica tell me that your lieing huh?"

"NO, no no, Rocky it's true, because I'm..."

Rocky suddenly slapped her across the face. He went crazy. "Veronica don't say that, don't ever say that again."

"Then, what eles am I susposed to say Rocky?" Veronica was screaming.

"I am pregant and..."

"No, no, no, shaddup you hear me." Rocky was showering her with a mass of voilent blow's. "Shaddup, Veronica cause your not what you just said you were. Your lieing. You hear me your lieing." He suddenly pushed her up against a wall. Veronica was screaming all the time. I thought he was goning to strangle her. Seth ran up to them suddenly makeing him back off. "Hey, Rocky just leave her alone huh."

Rocky swung around, suddenly pushing him off. He swiped Seth across the face. "Your a bastard. Your the one who raped her. You did all that behind my back? You had the gut's to do all that stuff while I was away?"

Seth shook his head. "No, no I did'nt Rocky."

"You did, your a cheat you did." Rocky suddenly pushed him back. He sent him flying into the backgammon table.

I yelled out at them both to stop. "Rocky leave him alone it is'nt his fualt."

"It's not my baby. You hear it's not my – baby."

"What's the good of arguing.." Screamed Veronica. "It's me the one who's pregant not you two."

Rocky suddenly swung around. He yelled out. "You broad, you whore, you cheap, you double-crossing lousy prostitue."

Veronica suddenly looked cool. She pulled back her hair. "Call me all the name's under the sun if you like. But Rocky the baby is your's."

Rocky suddenly went quite. He went up to her. His dark form looking ridged in the darkness. "Jesus god I would sooner kill you than, let you say that." His voice came through clenced teeth. "You had the lousy, cunningness to fuck your ass around all those guy's." He summarly shot out his hand, and struck her across the face.

Veronica screamed out. "It's not true. You just won't listen to me."

"I don't wanna listen to you."

"Rocky the baby is – your's."

"The baby is not mine, cause you lie."

"No, no, I'm telling the truth."

"Veronica no, you listen to me. I'm not stupid, and I know that you've been haveing it with somebody other than me."

"Like who then?"

"Like a lousy, lowdown cunt."

"That's not true."

"It is true."

"No we had sex that day I remember."

"What day?"

"Rocky the baby is YOUR'S."

Rocky summarly threw up his arm's. He almost kicked down the door as he struggled to open it. His face was bearly visable, as he yelled out to her summarly: "Then your gonna pay for it." The door slammed loudly shut. It sent a vibration of steaming anger around the room. Veronica did'nt do anything for a moment. She stood stareing at the door. I could'nt make out the expression on her face. Then she suddenly headed into the direction of the bathroom, with her hand's extending her face. Seth picked himself up from the floor. Not saying a word, neither did I and neither did Daltyboy, who I decided had just completly fallen asleep. I stared carefully through the darkness at the scatterd remain's of the backgammon peice's, my mind thinking that I had just truly awoken from a bad dream.

Rocky did'nt come back that night, and so we just sat listening to the radio. We finally fell asleep around midnight. Then sometime around dawn Rocky suddenly came back without the slightest give away on his expression that anything so dramatic had just happened. He just stepped back in the pad, with a kinda happy smile on his face, swooped Veronica into his arm's, gave her a fire-cracking kiss on the lip's and then I guess thing's finally got back to normal, at last. Nobody we later found, could bring themselve's to talk about the pregnancy, not even Veronica, so I reckon after awhile we forgot about it all.

Rocky quit his job for a few day's and we just sat around doing our usual dig's. We did'nt talk much. But on the fifth day Rocky suddenly came up with something. "Hey, listen you guy's why'nt we have some kind of a disco. I could just put on some record's, and we could just dance. How about that?"

"Yeah, well why not." Seth agreed. He had already just simply forgivend Rocky for what he had acused him about the previous night. So had we all I guessed. Becuase up to now neither of us could have beleived that Rocky was capable of bringing around such a dramatic performance.

"I reckon it'll be a rest away from the real thing."

"Swell." Said Rocky.

In a while he had the whole pad alive with music. We danced in something like a moonlighted She-bang because haveing to pay the electricty bill was becoming something more of a burden for Rocky. The only one who did'nt really dance was Veronica. She sat gazing out infront of her instead without the slightest notion into what we were doing.

"Hey, Veronica your not dancing how not?" Rocky had quit dancing. He stood watching her through the candle light. Then went to sit by her.

The lyric's to the record blared across the room. They sent vibration's cracking around the wall's, and all in all they blotted out the sempiternal yapping that had been going on for age's in the pad nextdoor to our's. Though it had been quite loud neither of us could figure out to what was been said. But I reckon it was just another lover's tiff, because whoever the voice's belonged to one was male, while the other female and they did'nt sound as if they were speaking on freindly term's, either.

"Dance with the boogie get down. cos boogie night's are alway's the best in town". Seth and I boogied to the music, with the candlelight flickering around the wall's, makeing the whole pad come alive with shaddow's. Even Daltyboy manged to throw away his comfortor, dancing with the music as though he had summarly come alive, with a new burst of engery. "Boogie night's get that groove, let it take you higher Boogie night's make it move set this place on fire."

"Hey, Rocky you got anymore of that paridise stuff." Seth sang out. "Cause I'm feeling I could do with a drag right now?"

"Yeah. Sure. Come over here." Rocky had stood up. He took out a crumpled package from the back of his jean's. Then he handed it to Seth. "Here, share them out to the rest to huh?"

"Yeah. sure." Seth ambled back to me, and then in a moment the room was cozy as we all sprawled ourself's along the floor, dragging away with simplicty at some marjuana ciggerate's. Rocky joined us in a while. So did

Veronica. She did'nt look too happy. But I thought to myself dreamingly: at least were all back together again. Then I said aloud: "Boy, I feel as sleepy as a log." And Seth dreamly put an arm around me, before saying sleeply. "Yeah. and... me too." Then we all took another drag of our wonderful... paridise, before finally hitting the sack.

It was warm and it was hot. But it was mostly hot, and I was laying peaceably on my own. With my eye's closed on a large, fluffy, bed of sand. The sun peeled herself slowly into my eye's. From somewhere there came a rich aroma of something cooking. I was figureing that it was only the heatwave, and that my mother together with Oscar were haveing themself's a glorious, beach-kind barbiecue.

Then there came the nearby sound of crackling paper. The aroma that now driffted around me was like the aroma of something haveing just been burnt. I weakly opened my eye's. Oh – it was so hot. My mother must have gone for a stroll and forgotten about the barbiecue. The sound of voice's reached my ear's. "Hey, man it's burning......." Yes the steak is burning. The steak has been burnt and so I guess our little barbicue has just been ruined. I wiped my hand across my hotly, wet forehead. Then I spotted with cloudy eye's a blackened face stareing down at me. "Oscar don't just stand there. The barbiecue is burning."

"Ca'nt you do anything about it?"

"The pad is burning Olivia get up."

"The.. the what is burning?"

"The pad, now c'mon we have to get outta here." It did'nt sound like Oscar's voice at all. Infact it was almost screaming. "The pad Olivia. The pad is on fire."

I was suddenly dragged to my feet. Now the sky had gone weirdly black and I could hardly see a thing.

"Okay. Os.. Oscar I'll just go save the steak." But afterall it was my mother's, and his fault. They should never have left the barbiecue. The sound's of high-pitched scream's, yell's filled my ear's. Flicking, flame's of fire shot up into the sky.

Somebody pushed past me. I was thrown back into reality, and: "Help." My god the pad was on fire. "Help we have to get outta here."

Daltyboy was coughing like mad. He stumbled around crazily. Then his comfortor was on fire. I ran to his rescue. I managed to pull away the comfortor. Then we found ourself's stumbling akwardly toward the door.

Seth and Rocky where nowhere to be seen. Then I heard a yell. "Quick... this whole place is gonna fall in."

Veronica was standing backing the window. The flame's were almost on her. "Veronica." She turned around. She was looking through the window. "Veronica C'mon we have to get outta here." I grabbed at her sleeve. But she did'nt move. "Veronica... please please hurry up." I was suddenly lost in a suffercateing pyxosam of coughing. I staggerd blindly into a wall. Seth had grabbed hold of Veronica, and he was pushing her toward the door. He grabbed my hand. Then we were all stagering, blindly like crazy toward the door. In a trial of gasping moment's we all managed to get ourself's down the step's. Then we were all collasped summarly on to the sidewalk. I was gasping for what seemed like age's before I finally caught my breath. The sky was black and the moon was bright, and I suddenly heard somebody scream. It was a long terrifying wail, and it was Veronica's. She was standing up franticly, crazly pointing toward the building. In a moment Seth was up and trying to calm her down. "Hey, Veronica it's okay.... just... take a hold... of yourself.. okay?"

She was struggling to get back into the building. Her band's franticly waveing through the air. Then above the sound of Daltyboy's deathly dying cough's I heard her scream's fill with something eles. She was'nt screaming she was yelling out somebodie's name. "R-O-C-K-Y-EEE."

"ROCKY!." Oh my god I swung around. I saw Daltyboy. There was nobody eles but Seth, Veronica and I.

"Seth." I summarly sprang from the sidewalk. "It's Rocky... It's Rocky he's missing."

Seth suddenly swung around. He let go of Veronica. She ran crazily back toward the building. He screamed after her. "Veronica come back.. you'll die.. comeback."

Her footstep's were bullet-like fast. I yelled out for her. "Veronica." The whole street was ablaze from the color of the red, hot fire. Flame's greedly licked around the apartment. There were sound's of running feet as people from all direction's came flying to ourside's. "What's doning? Hey is there anybody still in there?" A voice yelled out.

My hand's flew to my face as Veronica crazily mounted the outside step's. She had managed to stagger through the doorway, when Seth suddenly lept on her. He pulled her back swiftly from the screaming mouth of the dragon. She was screaming all the time. Seth was halfway to pushing her onto the side walk.

When he suddenly swung back around and ran back up the step's. "No, Seth. No." I screamed.

Veronica was yelling out. "He has to save Rocky. . Rocky's in there. He has to save him."

I ran sumarly out into the street. "Seth.. Seth come back." The apartment was burning like an inferno. It was just like a hell. Seth was backing his way swiftly through the doorway. His arm's wrapped tightly across his head. I stopped and yelled out for him. "Seth.. come back.. please." He would die in there. He was about to die. There was a sudden yell from him. Then he was running back into the street.

"Olivia... Olivia it's.. no use. I can't get in there."

"Seth you don't have... to be a.. hero." I yelled. "You.. don't have.. to be a hero.. I only want.. you to live." I threw my arm's around him. Seth was coughing like crazy. Veronica screamed out. "What about Rocky. ROCKY.. what about Rocky... Seth... Seth you have to save him."

I swung around to see Veronica makeing her way back to ward the building. But Daltyboy had grabbed hold of her. He was coughing and she was trying to break free. The sound of screeching fire-engine's filled my ear's. They came to a stop right outside the building.

Seth yelled out: "I could'nt see him. I could'nt see him."

The sound of crazy crackling filled the street. Part's of the building were dropping with fire to the street. We were staggering blindly down the sidewalk. Spraying water splashed against the angrey flame's. Veronica was still crying out. Hord's of people flocked the area. They yelled out, waveing franticly at the storming volcano. It was like hour's before we found ourself's finally collasped onto a peice of grass verge. Daltyboy coughed madly for thirty second's his face was more white than black at that moment. It was light where we sat. I caught my breath heavly with my heart pounding like crazy. Seth was sprawled out on his back, and Veronica was still wailing out, though it was more to herself. "Rocky.. we ought to.. have saved Rocky."

A ringing ambulance screeched around the corner. Veronica slowly stood up her hand's locked tightly together. "I know he's still alive.. I know... it."

We must have been sitting there, catching our breath's for at least half an hour before, through the moonlight we could identify a dark figure comming our way. My heart did a crazy leap. Seth stood up. He was pointing madly down the street. But he could'nt say anything. The way that figure walked. The outline of that macho frame. I rose to my feet slowly. All the time my mouth hanging wide open. Then I suddenly yelled with joy: "My god, halliluia it's Rocky."

"Holy jesus this is worse than the living dead." Yelled Seth. He suddenly staggerd of the sidewalk.

Rocky came running toward us. His face, his arm's, his clothe's, his hair, all as black as the snow is white. He stared at us all wildly. Then he said lowly: "Okay, which one of you crazy breadnut's is responsible for leaving your ciggerate alight?"

"Well it was'nt me." We all chorused, as we all looked around at each other bewilderingly.

"And then so." Rocky slowly, carefully broke into a lopsided grin. "It was'nt me eiether." He angled his thumb to his chest, and we all suddenly broke into a crazy round of yelling laughter. Hugging all over him as we did. It was he who quit laughing first, because he was suddenly looking at Veronica. She was standing some way a way. Her hand's still tightly clasped together. The two remained gazeing at each other for what seemed an enternity before Veronica finally said: "Last night I stubbed my ciggerate out."

Rocky smiled and just shrugged his shoulder's. Somewhere around me there came this almost spooky feeling that Veronica had just said something totally eerie. I don't know if the rest had felt it. But I certainaly had. It was like Veronica had been suddenly reading our mind's. "Are you okay?" Rocky prolonged his gaze.

Veronica lowered her head. "I wanna go home."

Rocky turned his head to both his shoulder's. The moon showed that the expression on his face was now anxious. "We have to get outta here." Something made him quit talking, then: "We all wanna go home."

He ambled down the street. I was thinking the same thing. I wanted to go home too. Seth yelled out. "Hey, everybody I wanna go home too."

Daltyboy joined him. "I wanna go home. I've had enough." I finally said it out loud. "I wanna go home too."

Rocky quit walking. Then turned around. "Right now there is this big, black cloud hanging right down over my head, you guy's. But I don't think were gonna make home – tonight. So why'nt we just hitch us a ride to Virginia?"

"West Virginia?" We choroused.

"West Virginia." Rocky dug into his jean's pocket. "You know why I almost died in that fire today? To give you all a good time cause the minute we touch Virginia I'm gonna give you a treat." In the moonlight.

In the palm of his hand lay what looked like a million dollar note's. "And I did almost die tonight. Cause I had to save some of this too."

He showed us a crumpled package of marijuana. "But I guess I'm born lucky, cause there is a backway through my pad and so, that's how I escaped from that flaming building, and I guess if I did'nt get out of that building when I got out. I would now be left to rot with all my gear back there. and where would that leave me huh?" He pointed skyward's. "Up there I guess."

We all nodded in agreement. Beside's where eles could Rocky have gone too? He was a hero, and all hero's go to heaven.

In about another five minute's we were all busy thumbing our way down the street. Altogether around a dozen truck's past us. I was thinking to myself summarly: whatever happened to the word kindness, when a truck did stop. It pulled up neatly by the kerbside. We all ran behind it and I heard somebody yell: "How high the moon." And that somebody was me.

This time the driver was accompanied by a passenger. His brown shag of hair was the same texture of his scatterd eyebrow's. He looked at us all mildly through the moonlight before saying: "Hi there kid's what kin I do you for?"

"It's alright. We only need a lift." Seth had spoke.

"Awright. then were you headed?" The driver briskly scratched his head.

"West Virginia."

"West Virginia, your kidding cause I'm only headed Oklahoma myself." The driver looked startled a moment. Then: "Okay kid's jump in around the back and make yourself's real at home, cause we have along way toggo."

We all ran like crazy to the back of the truck. Just feeling glad that at last we had managed to flag down a ride. It was one of those open air back's. So I reckoned as the truck began to pull out onto the road, that we could just lay back, enjoy the ride and basically if we liked just fall asleep under the shining moon, and the gleaming star's. It was a pretty hot night atucally. But Daltyboy sitting alongside Rocky and Veronica looked about as cold as stone. His knee's were tightly propped up, his arm's wrapped stiffly around his shoulder's, and his head was bowed deeply into his chest. This was'nt the hibernateing season. But he did look as though he was, and I was'nt actually too keen on parting with my sweat-shirt either. I mean as well as it was a hot night. I figured it would mean me freezing to zilch if I parted with my extra skin, too. Maybe it was just because it happened to be night, instead of daytime and that we were now travelling around at least 50 mile's an hour across the highway. Veronica and Rocky appeared to be enjoying the journey, however even if they were both apparently asleep, with their head's resting on top of each other, and their arm's slightly linked.

My head collasped summarly onto Seth. His shoulder was right now the perfect pillow and I soon found myself cozyily floating away into never-never land.

An alarming clamor of what sounded like a terrific mountain of crashing pot's and pan's filled summarly through my ear's as I struggled to open my eye's. It was morning, the sun was just about come alive and we were still racing along the highway in the back of a pick up truck. A thousand automobil's, speed buggie's and orinary truck's were already on the road. In a moment all of us had awoken. "Hey you guy's we'er still on the highway." My voice was barely a croak.

"Yeah I know." Seth yawned tuckerd. "And I have'nt slept two year's." Rocky streached out his arm's. He looked dead. "Hey, I feel dead.. I feel as though I've been running up a mountain." He brushed his hand's tiredly over his face, as Daltyboy beside him summarly strected his leg's out. An over takeing truck load of hay, spraying us with it's left over's had Veronica more than awake in no time. She struggled wildly with her hair before it finally quit makeing her have the dishevlled aspect of a scarecrow. "Gee, I'm hopeing the queen can't see me now." She swiftly plasterd her hair down to her scalp.

A matter of moment's passed. The truck arubtly pulled into the sisde of a layby. "That's as far as ya'll go kid's." The driver's voice rang out in the cool morning air. We were stationed someplace in the corner of a town. Jumping out from the truck made us all feel like we were sky doveing from a 90 foot skyscraper.

"Well I sure hope's y'all will reach ya destination real quick."

"Thank's for the ride." Seth held his thumb up. "We sure appreaciate it."

"Yeah right on." The driver held up his thumb. "And see if yah kin pay a little vist to ma old woman when ya git's to Virginia – she live's up in a place named Cedar Creek, has a real big ranch ya know's and it'll be a real blessing if she git's to meetin some young folk like y'all."

The driver restarted the engine. Then smiling he handed Seth a dollar note. "Heh, take dat do ya a world of good."

Seth shrugged before takeing it. "We don't really need it that bad but..."

"Lotsa kid's would be sayin them thing's." The driver chuckled. "I'm jist hard sorry, I can't be takin y'all all the way in – Anyhow's solong freind's." He waved. The truck pulled into the road, leaveing a faint cloud of Oklahoma dust to cover our sneeker's. It was a short while before we said anything. From overhead could be heard the sound's of chirping bird's as they made their way across the turquise sky's. I ambled around stifly. My eye's takeing in all the unfamilura town scenary.

It was like we had been planted inside a western movie box. From the left side of our ear's came the sound of a jingling bell, followed by the far sound of a bellowing cow. I breathed deeply takeing in the rich smeel of country air, before I summarly put on my high rich Texen accent:

"Man, don't the maze smell good?"

"Don't it smell ripe?" Put in Rocky. "It make's me feel good to be a country boy." He ambled around hautily as though he were hitching up a pair of overall strap's. The cracking sound of laughing geese filled our ear's. I walked around with my head held high.

"Heh, I jist about forgit to put on ma overall's!" Seth anounced. "Cause this here land is real Texen beauty." He sniffed the air wildly.

Daltyboy had just about recoverd from his dead leg's. He looked around better already. "Man is this air doing me a world of good."

"Gee I could stay here forever and a day." Veronica twirled around lightly sending her mass of titian hair flying through the air. "I jist forgot to bring ma little, cute corn dolly that's all."

Oklahoma I reckoned, as I took another breath of it's air, had me takeing to it just like a fish does to water.

We ambled down the dusty road, my mind still telling me that we had to be in some kinda of western movie house. A man clad in, neck tie, check shirt and denim overall's ambled by us tagging along behind him a grey and brown, hefty stallion. He raised his eye's, tilting his head slightly as we past him by. Row's of maze filled truck's lined the sandy street's. Dozen's of stranger's either sitting outside store house's with blade's of hay sticking away from their mouth's, or chatting to freind's as they helped to unload their stack's of maze, eyed us all warily as we ambled in down the street. Looking around we saw drink bar's, row's of candy-lined store's, a warehouse that was packed with all kind's of wooden mementoe's, chiaware and colorful dressed corn doll's, a drugstore that looked as though it only sold whisky and ciggerate's and a huge clutter of store's that had written neatly on one door:

"C'MON Y'ALL N'EAT OUR COUNTRY CORN."

We were walking down the street just peeking in around and out of these storehouse's when a big hearty "Hi there stranger's." Made us all summarly swing around. Looking down at us from what seemed like a big wide stetson hat, and a mass of neatly trimmed bushy eyebrow's was the tallest man one could ever set eye's on in a place as countrystyle as this.

Infact he was wearing a steston, together with a red polka dot neck tie and a green check shirt. Not forgetting the overall's, which altogether did look like they could fit a giant, if not a drawf. His face looked pretty red from the sun, and slightly plump. "Ain't ya about lookin for ma big pretty wife Annie?"

I did'nt actually know what he was talking about. Neither I guess did the other's. "Annie?"

"Yep, Annie. She's ma wife an she's jist git about the biggest caffitaria running around here, if y'all go there now ya bound ta git the biggest break-fast of yah life's."

"Which way do we head?" Seth asked, still a little taken back by this large hunk of a texen.

"Aw. Well ya jist go long dis street here, turn direction long dah drug store, walk up a couple of yard's long dah blacksmith, turn in to dah little ally dat run's longside dah schoolbarn... an ya should then be standin right outside of ma big Annie's cafeteria." He angled an arm up into the direction of yet another kind of drugstore. "So nah y'all jist go up there an prolong ma route awright?"

"Yeah. sure. thank's alot." We chorused, and we ambled up the street like our big stranger had told us to. He then chuckled for a moment before crossing back across the street.

The caffeteria, when we had at last found it, was infact kinda big. It had the name "Annie" splashed across one of the window's, and the sound of Dolly Parton's rich country voice rang out from the doorway as she sang her song "Jolene".

We picked a small, red checked coverd table by the window. It was'nt all that crowded. A group of beer drinking guy's sat alongside the bar just talking while they listened to the radio. In a while one of them ambled over with a deep smile on his face. "Heh, you headed someplace kid's?" He slowly leaned an elbow across the table. "Cause I have a truck out there if ya like."

Seth nodded his head. "Yeah, West Virginia."

A loud high laugh came from one of the guy's by the bar. It was followed by the rest imeadiatlly joining in.

"Well, look, listen kid's y'all eat ya breakfast an I'll be waitin for ya when ya finished okay?"

"Okay." Seth looked around at us, before shrugging his shoulder's. The blonde headed guy stood straight. He yanked a glance over his shoulder at the bar. "Heh, Annie ya there, C'mon give each these kid's here somethin ta eat an drink."

A tall, plump, blonde haired woman with a teacloth slumped across her shoulder came from behind a door, her hand's resting firmly on her hip's. She smiled slightly when she saw us. I thought she looked rather like another Dolly Parton. "Ask them if dey kin pay for ma meal?"

The blonde guy tossed his head. "Aw woman jist go git dah eat's huh? I'll be payin ya for dah meal's, have them something nice like ya beautiful baked cookie's an ya doubled fryed bean's with plenty cawfee okay?"

Annie tossed her head, with a smile and disapeard behind the door. The cloth now dangling from her hand.

In a moment she appeared again carrieing a large tray, steaming with black coffee and loaded with a Texenstyle breakfast. "Here ya go." She ambled up to us, placeing the tray down on to the table.

The blonde headed guy took out a five dollar note and placed it in her open plam. "Annie's gonna git her gun." He said as she smiled, and ambling back toward the bar. A high laugh erupted from the group beside the bar, she flicked at one of them with her cloth. Then disapeated back behind the door, from where the rich smell of cookie's and coffee drifted out from the cafeteria.

We ate the meal while the guy went over to sit back with his freind's.

Then it was like a moment, before we were sitting in the back of his truck getting ready to leave for West Virginia. His name was Carson Tennessee, because that was what all his freind's had been addressing him as he jumped into his seat. "Heh, Billy there." He called over to an oversall clad guy ambling up the street. "Ya wanna ride, cause I'm aheaded West Virginia right now?"

The guy nodded his head, running and jumped into the passenger seat. "Seem's like a long time, I've bin up ta Virginia ma old pa'll be worrin bout me too." He said. Then he turned around, waveing at us through the small back window before the truck pulled out into the street and we were headed back for the highway, with loud yell's of: "So long buddie's." And "It's bin nice meetin ya kid's." echoeing out behind us.

With us all in the back of the truck was an old steel guitar. I studied it for a while, before decideing to examin it, and see if the string's were still playable enough. An oveertakeing pickup truck whizzed by, blowing my hair into a dissary. I was peaceably thinking about my home again. Way back there in L.A., and now we were headed to West Virginia. As I slowly placed the guitar underneath my arm's, I was feeling like the girl Dorthy from the: "Wizard of oz." She had just simply clicked her little red shoe's together, and wished that she was home sweet home and then she had been home. Maybe the same would work for me if I was to simply click my sneaker's together.

Tranging one of the guitar string's I began to sing quitely to myself.

"Country road's take me home
to the place I belong
West Virginia
mountain mama
take me home
country road's.

Almost heaven
West Virginia
blue ridge mountain
shine in the river
Life is old there
older than the tree's
younger than the mountain's
blowing like a breeze."

Everybody was watching me as I sang and everybody joined in with the chorus. We sang wide and clear into the open country air.

"Country road's take me home
to the place I belong
West Virginia
mountain mama
take me home
country road's."

I sang clearly by myself while Seth clapped his hand's motioning to Rocky, Veronica and Daltyboy to do the same. They clapped and I sang as clear as I could.

"All my memorie's
gather round her
finest lady
stranger to blue water
dark and dusty

Painted on the sky
missed the taste of moonshine
tear drop in ma eye.

"Take me home
country road's
to the place I belong
West Virginia
mountain mama
take me home
country road's.

I here her voice in the morning
how she call's me
The radio remind's me of ma
home far away and driving
down the road I get a feeling
that I shouda bin home
yesterday – yesterday.

"Country road's take me home
to the place I belong
West Virginia mountain mama
take me home country road's."

As we all sang the last few line's the blue siren of a police car rumbled by. I tranged on the guitar and we all continued to sing. The two guy's in the front singing and clapping with us.

"Country road's take me home,
take me home country road's
take me home country road's
take me home country road's"

We were all rooting for each other's when we finally finnished the song.

Then Rocky summarly waved his arm up the highway to where as clear as missippi mud the police car was parked, waiting for somebody in a nearby layby. "Hey, everybody don't you think we oughta fly the coop?" Rocky was already makeing to quit the truck. I put away the guitar, while Seth called out to Calson Tennesse to quit driveing. He pulled up some yard's behind the car. "Heh, nah y'all what's hurrin ya?.. cause dat sure was some nice country singin ya did back there."

"Were kinda sorry." I annonced as we all jumped down from the back of the truck. "We have to go right now. But we sure appreciate you for the ride. It was swell."

Up along the highway not only was there a police car. But now a whole patrol stood parked awkwardly along the end. I did'nt know what the hold up exactly meant. Seth, Veronica, Rocky, Daltyboy and I though just got out of that jam fast. There stood one of the cop's, holding up his hand as though to prevent the traffic getting by. For that matter us too.

We scuttled along behind the train of stalling truck's. I almost tripped over my sneaker's as we made it behind a tree. We slipped into some murky hide of woodland, Daltyboy coughing all the way. it was then that we quit running to catch our breath's.

"You know something... I don't think those cop's were after us." It was Seth who spoke. He hung desperately onto a tree.

"Oh yeah, then why did we run?" Rocky flung a look at him. "Think we would've ran if they we'rnt after us?"

"I did'nt say they were after us. What I said is that I don't think their after us."

I did'nt actually know which one to believe at this point. All cop's have that hardened aspect as though they need to catch somebody: throw just anybody who's inocent enough into the joint. I thought the air of Oklhoma was beginning to smell rather foul, or wherever we were. I did'nt have a tiny dime, except that we were in a peice of woodland; on the run from a bundle of cop's who thought themselve's clever enough to track down a tribe of runaway kid's. I turned to glance behind me, then at Seth. "You figure they followed us all from L.A.?"

Seth shrugged his shoulder's. "I'm no geneious."

Daltyboy began to cough again. He quit almost arubtly when we all heard a rustling in the bushe's. "Hey, what was that?"

"Don't ask us." Rocky whirled around. His hand's were raised to the sky. "But ask the lord cause I think it's rain."

"Rain?"

"Uh huh – rain."

"Well come back another day, huh." I was'nt all into getting my clothe's drenched; neither could I see was Daltyboy. He looked kinda sicker than ever. "Can't we get back on the highway? This place is giving me the creep's."

Veronica began to wail like a siren. I thought: we could do without another one. Rocky turned to her. He put his arm's around her shoulder's. The rain began to fall like a waterfall. "Christ what should we do? Pray the lord to quit the rain, or let it give us all a nice long shower?"

He said this tonno body inpaticular. We had all ran to shelter underneath some row's of branche's. Seth, Daltyboy and I sat huddled in what seemed like a gigantic tree hollow, surrounded by mass's of thick branche's. Daltyboy was coughing perpetually.

"Hell, this is worse than a monsoon." Seth snapped his finger's. "I was thinking only we were in Nashville someplace. But what difference is that gonna make?"

I shrugged my shoulder's under a shower of spraying rain. "You sure.." A loud thunder of rain cut me short. "That were.." Another outburst of rain.

"In Nashville?"

"Yeah as sure as the rain come's down."

By the time we had washed our way out of that woodland Ray Bradbury's book was showering in my mind, Golden apple's of the sun, in which we were supposed to find some kinda dome. Though we did'nt unfortunately so we were pretty much drip-washed to the bone's. Daltyboy got hit by it the worse. He was really coughing. Loud enough; dangerous enough to let anybody think he had only a few second's to live. We were back on a highway. Not exactly a highway. But a little dusty dirtroad. Seth had his tee-shirt in his hand. He was practicly useing it as a towel. I thought; we all right now needed a towel.

"Hey. so where should we head?" His voice sounded a mere crack. "Wherever the road take's us." Rocky decided.

"Yeah, well we've already tried that, look where we've ended up."

The sky seemed summarly clear again. Just how long had we been in that Woodland. Long enough I thought for Daltyboy to suddenly collaspe to the ground from sheer exahauston, "Hell – I can't even breath." He had his hand pressed tightly over his chest. Wheezly he began to cough again. I dropped to my knee's beside him. He was really on his death bed.

"Daltyboy are you alright?"

"Don't ask dumb question's, how can I be." He gasped. He coughed violently before getting into a real fit. It was like he had gone delirious. He had gone delirious. He was writhering around on the ground like a wounded snake. I wrecked my brain's for an positive answer.

"We'll have to get him to hospital."

"To a hospital." Seth made that statement almost arubtly, emphizing the A, as he did. "Cause A hospital is what – we – have to find."

"Okay, we'll find a hospital." I stood up searching the area as though indeed a hospital would spring up from the ground. Then I ran a little way up the road. Seth and Rocky had already picked Daltyboy up. They had his arm's slung around their neck's as they struggled to keep up the journey. We were walking just as lost as the crew from "The wizard of oz" when summarly to our great eye's there came a faint rumbling noise from behind us. I swung around imeadiately to see a large, dusty grey truck headed ourway. Could the lord truly be on our side? We were about to get to a hospital afterall. I almost clapped with joy as Veronica and I ran back down the road. The truck kept coming toward us. Then it stopped as the driver a large, burly man with a brown sun tanned face saw us both. By that time we had said about all the important thing's under the sun. "Yeah, well." He said. "There's a little hospital somewhere's down Stone's River."

"How far from here?" I asked.

"Aw, bout a stone's throw, why you need great help."

"Great help."

"Like we said Daltyboy our buddy, now he's real sick." Veronica pointed down the road to where Seth, and Rocky were just about keeping him alive.

"Jump in." The driver threw open the door. Veronica and I jumped in. We drove a little way along the road to where the other's were waiting. Then the driver quit; jumped out. He easily helped Daltyboy into the back of the truck. Seth and Rocky jumped in beside him. Then we were rumbling up the road again. "How bad did ya say ya buddy was?"

"I think he has phemiono." I could hear him coughing like crazy in the back, jesus was he in trouble.

"Think he'll last out till we get to ta hospital?"

"Uh huh. I hope so."

"Has he ever had a fit like this before?"

"It's only because he got wet a couple of week's back."

"And he has'nt been addmitted to a hospital yet?"

I shook my head slowly. "No." And I was thinking that all a long we should have. We should have realized that Daltyboy had been really sick. No he had'nt only been brought down by something like the flu. Because now he had something far worse than that. He had phemonia or was it bronchitist. But they were both the same. They were both dangerous I thought. Both dangererous enough to put an end to enternity.

The hospital when we found it, was'nt exactly standing inside of a river but it was pretty big actually. The driver pulled up just a few yard's away from the huge, glass framed door's. We were in Tennesee. The word's "Tennesse general Hospital." Stood out clearly against the whitewashed building of the hospital. I jumped out of the truck with Veronica. Seth, Rocky and the driver were already helping Daltyboy down. In a moment a couple of blue uniformed Nurse's came running from the building. Daltyboy was more than just a sick pateint. He was crictical. He was gasping for breath. My heart pounded inside of me as on a strecther he was carried in by a team of amberlance men.

"I think y'all have a real sick buddy there." The driver stood beside us. We were lost in a strange kinda daze as we stood watching him been carried away. Daltyboy our best buddy was really a sick kid.

"We appreacitate you for.. for the ride." Seth summarly looked up at the driver. As he did I was thinking, this guy had to be a samaritan. He was more than just a stanger to us. He had actually given us some luck. Daltyboy, just in time was going to be saved.

'Yep well I'm sorry kid's. But I gotta get along now." He had jumped back into the driver's seat. Though he did'nt look at though he wanted to leave us. "I have my work to see to down at the farm."

I tried to smile as he started up the engine. "Thank's anyway's. The ride was really helpful."

Rocky looked as though he were about to give him a dollar for his kindness. When instead he said: "I reckon the lord work's in mysterious way's cause we would still be back there I guess if you did'nt help us along."

The driver summarly grinned. "That's right kid's thank the lord not me. He's the one who make's all the wonder's, n all the mirclcal's come true."

He studied us all for awhilebefore saying: "How would ya like it if I let ya'll come long n stay at my place for a while, ya know just till your young buddy get's better."

Seth had almost suddenly shook his head. "No. Really. It's okay, our buddy's real sick and we'd like to stick around a little, you know just incase... incase he get's really bad."

"Huh, okay I understand." The driver smiled breifly. Then waved his hand amically as he drove out away from the hospital. He hooted his horn, twice before disapearing up behind a corner.

We looked at Seth for a moment before he said slowly: "That guy was kind. But it would'nt have been kind if we had left Daltyboy behind. He dosn't even know this place."

Rocky nodded his head. "Yeah, your right."

I thought about Daltyboy nervously. My heart pounding like a thunderbird.

"You think we oughta go in now and see him?"

"Hey, did you see the way that guy was carried in – I don't think he's fit to see anybody. He's that bad." Seth was gazing out at the building as he spoke.

Veronica was doing the same. Her face was written over with a picture of powerful anxitiy, as she hastily wrung her finger's.

"We ought to go in. Just to sit in the waiting room."

Her voice worked like magic. It was so watery. We were in the building in no time. The waiting room, though it was really crowded we did'nt seem to regonize the gloomy bunch of men, women and children. We just sat; waited for what seemed an enternity before a nurse came in and looked at us. Her brown hair was done up neatly; it was hiddened by a blue cap. "Are you the realative's of the sick boy?"

"Yeah.' Seth stood up. "Freind's really but he's just like a blood brother to us."

The nurse studied us throughly before saying: "The boy is still desperately ill. But there is a small chance that he'll pull through."

The nurse looked at us now almost sternly. "Did'nt you know that he suffer's from asthma?"

It was like she was suddenly talking about another pateint. Daltyboy suffering from asthma? He had never mentioned it to us. It was impossible. We had never heard him wheeze before. Never really seen him layed up dangerously sick by it. He had danced in the disco's like all the other kid's. Infact he had been really healthy. But then I thought sumarely: up to now. Only up to now had he seemed perfectly normal, and now this nurse had come up with something that neither of us had ever known. All of us shook our head's liflessly, because we just could'nt beleive on what the nurse had just told us.

"You did'nt, well I'm afraid he has. Like I said there can only be a small chance that he'll ever pull through."

"Will – will it be okay if we go see him?" I asked. My voice sounding really weak. The nurse shook her head.

"I'm sorry, but that can't be till the mornin, your freind is very, very sick." She ambled away from us summarely. Her attention haveing been called on by somebody eles. "I'm sorry Mr and Mrs Mcmillan, but you'll just have to wait untill your son come's out from the operateing theater." An elderly couple sitting somewhere across the room were both looking just as anxiously sad as we were. I ran my finger's through my hair not knowing that we were to hit the sack in that very same spot.

The sun shone gleamingly through the window. It was morning. We had been sitting waiting, in the waiting room all night. I thought we must have fell asleep because all of us were now just opening our eye's. I felt stiff. But the new pain soon came hurling back to me that Daltyboy was desperately sick. He was in a serious condition. A nurse came in as I stood up. She was carring a tray of cup's. "A cup of coffee for the early bird's?" The tray was placed down ontop of the small table which contained various ash tray's; ciggerate butt's.

"Is he okay?" I asked.

"You shan't be able to see him today. His condition is crittical." The nurse conveyed an expression of extreme regret.

"When do we get to see him?" Seth asked.

"That is for him to decide. Maybe when your freind has the strenght to say something he'll mention you alright?"

"Yeah. okay."

When she left. We noticed summarly how empty the room was. I was thinking of the elderly couple who were in here last night. Whether they had got to see their son. Takeing a sip of my coffee I also had the funny feeling that I had done this before. Veronica had run off to find the washing facuilty's. Been sick every morning was now a familular costom to her. Rocky looking as though he had'nt slept a wink got up. He ambled toward the window. Before saying sleeply: "Last night I had this weird dream."

Seth studied him. "Yeah, about what?"

"Daltyboy. us and this whole crazy life were leading."

"Was it nice."

"No it was a nightmare." Rocky turned to face us. "But I did'nt get to see the end of it."

"That's what dream's are for." I said. "Maybe."

Rocky nodded. "Cause it's sometime's fatel to see what's gonna happen at the end of a nightmare."

When the coffee had been drank. It was decided that we should go out take a walk on the hospital ground's. Neither of us had the proper strengh to converse, so it was a peaceful, silent walk.

It was with a deadpan expression and a low ugent voice that a nurse summond us to come in. We ambled hastily to her. Just haveing completed our tenth round outside the hospital.

"He'll be needing you now." The nurse pointed toward a corrider. "He's in one of the private ward's. Six."

I ambled down the corrider hastily with the other's with the word's; "you shan't be able to see him today. His condition is crittical." Looming phantasmly in my head.

When we reached Daltyboy's ward a cold chill went down my back. He looked as though he was on his deathbed. White drawn face, weakly closed eye's and his bluish lip's slightly parted as though in need of air. Seth went to sit by his bedside. I pulled up a chair doing the same. Veronica and Rocky stood over us their expressions no more lamented than our's. Daltyboy did'nt open his eye's.

Seth touched him gently on his arm which lay uncoverd ontop of the comforter's. Then weakly his eye's opened. A small whisper dominated the room. "Hi.. buddie's."

Seth and I spoke at the same time. "Hi."

"When... do.. I get... outta.. here?"

"It's okay pal were here with you." Seth had took his hand in his. Now he squeezed it tightly. Daltyboy responded by smiling briefly.

"Hey, Daltyboy?" Rocky's voice cracked. "I had this weird dream about you last night."

Daltyboy smiled again. "I've... alway's... been.. dreaming about.. you –." He gasped suddenly. Then broke up into a spasm of coughing. Seth held onto his hand tighter. Then he summarely stopped. "It's... alway's been... dream's.. that.. made.. me feel happy."

"Daltyboy we've sure been worried about you." Veronica's voice sounded watery. She sat down on the end of his bed. "But don't worry cause your going to get better and feel happier soon."

Daltyboy closed his eye's. His face seemed to go whiter. Turning his head, his cheek resting on the pillow he opened them again.

"Daltyboy, hey c'mon your not tired?" Seth asked him anxiously. Daltyboy closed his eye's again. His lip's parting wider than before.

"Daltyboy?"

"I feel fine."

"Hey, do you rembember when we first met Daltyboy?" Seth voice was suddenly full of humor. "It was a hot summer's day and school was almost over. We just saw you standing outside that candy store and we thought, boy will he do our gang a favor. Less than no time you were one of us and your face did'nt look so glum either. cause you were happy. So happy that your still here with us today.."

Daltyboy opened his eye's. "Do you.. love.. me?"

"We love you like a brother."

He smiled. "Thank's."

The room was silent for a moment. Daltyboy's eye's suddenly widen. He was looking straight infront of us as though he had just seen something truly wonderful. Then he whisperd slowly. "Please.. open the.. window's." Veronica sprang up and threw them open. A long cool summery breeze drifted in.

Daltyboy inhaled deeply as he smiled. His eye's rested on us all curiosly. "Did.. you.. keep.. my present's, buddie's.. huh?"

"I still have my doll." I said. "She was beautiful, she still is."

"Yeah and I still have my fantastic action man." Rocky laughed. "Though I think one of my kid brother's have got it by now.. Jesus brother's."

Veronica smiled wildly as she said: "That little teddybear, oh it was so cute Daltyboy I wish I had brought him with me, then I could take him with me wherever I went."

Daltyboy was smiling weakly. But suddenly sadly. "My parent's... they gave me.. everything.. except.. a family.. they.. never gave me.. any sister's.. or brother's." The room went silent again. Daltyboy turned his head to look at Seth. "You.. still have my chain?"

Seth nodded. "Yep." He put his finger's around his neck, uncliping it and held it out to Daltyboy.

Daltyboy smiled again. Happier. "It'll alway's.. remined you.. of me huh?"

"Alway's." Seth clipped it back on and held Daltyboy's hand again with more strengh. "Because it's sliver and it's beautiful."

"Hey, right... stay sliver Seth."

"You bet."

"Whadder. you.. guy's gonna.. be when you get.. old.. are.. you still gonna.. be bad?"

We all shrugged. Daltyboy smiled. His eye's rested on us. Then on Seth. Seth smiled. "I don't know. but I guess if your with us you can bet on us been a group of old dogooder's."

"Do.. me a.. beautiful.. favour Seth?"

"Uh huh I'll do anything."

"Give.. me a.. kiss."

Seth did'nt hesitate. But he just bent forward, giving Daltyboy a kiss on the cheek like he had requested.

"Thank's." The room went silent for a moment. With the cool summer breeze blowing across our face's. Daltyboy closed his eye's weakly. He smiled opening them again. "I'll.. believe that.... cause... only.... the good.... die... young..". His hand had gripped Seth's now so strongly. Then his eye's suddenly flutterd. He closed them again weakly. Seth almost jumped as Daltyboy turned his head and twicted slightly.

"That was beautiful Daltyboy, you'll be a poet someday."

I ran my hand slowly, carefully alongside his face. Daltyboy looked so young. He was peaceful. His expression like that of a sleeping baby. Seth had gone deadpan. He was slowly easing Daltyboy's clenched hand from around his. The tear's reached my eye's as he had to put up one last struggle. Freeing himself form the desperate, lifeless grip.

The door opened. A nurse came in quietly followed by a doctor. They didn't say anything. They were silent like us. Seth layed Daltyboy's hand back across his stomach. Over the comforter. Like before. "Die young. stay pretty." He whisperd.

The nurse stepped forward. "I'm sorry. But Dalton know it was comming." The name stung my ear's. Dalton. It was his real name. But we had nick named him Daltyboy. Alway's though I knew that Daltyboy was the name to be rememberd. Daltyboy Verrzano.

As we ambled out from the breezy peaceful room I had a sudden vision of Season. I turned back around. I knew that wherever Daltyboy had gone he was truly with her. Now they had been reunited.

The nurse shook her head again. "So sorry."

The doctor did the same. He was gazing regretably over at Daltyboy.

"Did he aks for his parent's?"

A blank shadow filled the air.

Seth wiped his eye's. He shook his head. "Because we were something more to him than that."

Standing outside of the hospital. We were all wearing the same sick, confused expression's. At first I could'nt bring myself around in believing what had happened. That Daltyboy had died. That we had seen him die. It was all so heart cutting. He was so young. Too young to die. Then I realized that he had died. Our live's would never be the same without him.

Heartbreaking a week driffted by. Oklhoma was left behind. There had seemed no reason to stay after Daltyboy's death because we did'nt know anything about funeral's in Olkhoma and we did'nt have that high feeling to face his parent's. So we left about two day's later. Now we were in San Francisco. We never made it to Virginia. It was as though we had flown from those large dusty plain's to the bright city light's in less than one hour. Rocky blew his monney, and although he had lost his job, and all his procession's none of those two lose's could cover the lost of a long term buddie.

"Okay everybody so what would you like?"

We were standing on a street corner. People of every color and size past us by. One of those day's when family's would most likly be found to have packed their lunch-case's and darted for the beach. I took the strand of hair that I had been sucking habitually for day's out from my mouth and I knew that my expression was deadpan: "Our best buddy back is the only thing that we would like."

A loud string of rumbling automobil's whizzed by. Veronica dejectedly like a lost child sat on the kerb of the sidewalk, her chin in her hand's.

"I wish that we had never been to Olkhoma."

"We did and now were in San francisco." Seth, his hand's pushed deeply into his jean's pocket's leaned against a doorway. It opened and he suddenly stumbled back.

"Hey, you guy's do me a big favor. Scram." A slim girl holding a broom stick in her hand with a mass of brown hair, twinkling eye's and a small heartshaped face stepped out from a doorway, after giving Seth a push in the right direction. "You have no bussness right here so go on now scoot." Then she closed the door. A second later it flew open again. And my god we had regonized each other at the same time.

"Jesus christ Olivia." She yelled.

"Pricilla." I could'nt believe my eye's after all these week's.

"What had you brought all the way down here?" Her broom dropped to the ground. She ran out to me. "My i'snt this luck meetin you here right outta the blue, your buddie's an all."

"Your not doing any more mugging's?"

"Uh uh." Her head slowly shook from one shoulder to the next. "Not any more cause I have this great monney grabbing job now."

"You know you have'nt changed a bit."

"Neither have you cause you look swell."

"Thank's. Meet my buddie's here."

"Hi." Seth held out a hand. "I'm Seth."

"Gee a real gentleman." Pricilla took and shook with him.

"And this is Veronica and Rocky."

"Hi there."

"Hi there."

Pricilla winked her eye at me. "You gotta real bunch of buddie's here."

"Thank's and so have you cause I did'nt really think that angry girl with the broom stick was you. Not Pricilla Slocum uh uh."

Pricilla laughed. "But Olivia Englewood this is you and.." She took my hand's in her's. "I'm so heart-happy that I met you." She stepped back inside of the store. Smiling at me as she did.

"I hope we meet up sometime again." I said.

"And I hope we meet up sometime again too, cause were real buddie's ain't that right?"

"Sure is."

Pricilla picked back up her broomstick. She winked her eye. "So long Olivia."

"So long Pricilla." The door closed. I waved and she waved back still smiling. Her eye's still twinkling in the sun light.

We ambled along the street. Seth looked at me asking: "Hey, who was that girl?"

"Pricilla Slocum. We shared a cell when we were in the joint."

Seth nodded. "Oh yeah, savvy."

In a moment we were standing outside of a large warehouse. “Hey, I don’t know a nickle about San Fransisco. But this look’s the place where we could buy something nice.” Rocky started to count the wad of dollar’s in his hand.

“Why waste monney?” Veronica did’nt seem to keen on reciveing a treat.

Her thought’s were eleswhere.

“I’m not. This is the treat I promised you. Remember?”

“No. I don’t need no treat anyway’s.” Veronica yawned. “I’m just tucked out that’s all.”

“C’mon Veronica.” I said linking my arm in her’s. “Maybe Rocky will buy us something to eat too. cause I’m starved.” Veronica nodded her head.

“Me too.”

It was crowded. People were everywhere. Though somehow we had managed to get inside the warehouse.

“Over here.” Rocky pointed to a stack of roller skate’s. “They look good huh?”

“What you want us to wear them?” Seth asked.

“Why not. They look terrific.”

“How much are they going to cost us?” My eye’s wonderd over to the shining stack. Maybe Rocky had gone crazy. But I thought why not buy a pair of roller skate’s?

“I done know. I’ll go ask this nice young assistant here.” The girl behind the cash desk with long black hair looked up smiling as Rocky approached her. “Excuse me how much are those skate’s over there please.” The girl looked around for a moment. She got up, ambling over to another assistant. Passed a few word’s. Then came back.

“Ten dollar’s, ninety nine cent’s.”

"Phew." Rocky almost stumbled back. "But okay I'll have four pair's please."

"If you'll please go get them then." The girl sat back behind the cash desk.

She held a surprized look on her face. Though she did'nt let it show too much. Rocky came back to us smiling. "Okay happy enough with your treat?"

"Happy enough." We all chourshed, breathlessly. We helped him to carrie the skate's over to the cash desk.

"Thankyou." The girl wrapped them all up. She began to calulate on the machine. Then Rocky handed her a wad of note's.

"Eighty dollar's seventy six cent's please."

Rocky dug into his pocket, produceing another dollar. He smiled then he passed us all a pair of the skate's.

Before we knew it we had put them on. Sitting along the sidewalk had proved to be quite a hazzard. Because whenever I was about to do up my strap somebody or some person's would trip over me and I would have to start all over again. Though in the end I managed successfully.

"Hey, you guy's where we headed?" Veronica asked.

They could'nt answer. Instead they were slip, sliding all over the place. I clung on to Veronica in my agony to keep standing. Otherwise I knew I would end up doing the bannana split's.

A moment later. Seeming more like 1 hour's all of us were free-whizzing down a crowded gangway. Though we wer'nt actually free-whizzing. But clinging onto the back's of each other's tee-shirt's instead, we were all having pretty much the same fun like we would inside of a crowded disco. About a dozen people must have been knocked flying by our crazy incounter.

Seth was the one who took lead. Twice he almost collided with a group of beatnik's. Twice we almost ened up like a heap of demolised brick's.

When we finally came to a skidding standstill, infact we were standing outside of a disco house, I thought we might go on whizzing forever. Seth hung onto a streetpost. He was breathing like a guy robbed of oxgen before he slid to the ground followed one by one by the rest of us.

"Hell that was some ride." He gasped later.

"No, it was more than hell, it was murder." Rocky decided. A passing automobil full of yelling kid's screeched to a standstill somewhere along the street. In a moment they all got out. A tall colored guy came toward us. "Hey, is this disco opened yet?" He asked.

"We don't know we just got here." Said Seth. He shrugged. The colored guy flicked his eye's over to the entrance. Like magic the door's were thrown open.

"Hey, c'mon you kid's it's open." He ran in followed by the group of stampeading kid's.

The music was blareing before we got the chance to pick ourself's up. "You know something I think this is a roller disco." Veronica pointed to a red flashing sign. It read "Everybodie's roller disco."

Inside kid's were slip, sliding all over the roller floor. "Shall we go ahead and dance in our skate's?" I asked resting my eye's firmly on the manger who was watching us suspiciously.

"Hey, why not?" Decided Rocky. "Cause I think we have to pay for the one's you get in here."

"That's right." The manger had jumped us. He looked down at our skate's crititally. "Have you payed for these one's."

Rocky answered: "Yeah."

"How come I never saw you go to the cash desk over there then?" The manger swung his arm over to the left. A queue lined up infront of a red headed lady were no doubt handing her some cash.

"Because these skate's here happen to be our's."

"Oh yeah, can you prove that?"

"Yeah. sure." Rocky produced a slip of paper from his pocket. The manger gazed at it. "You brought them all from Madison's cash an carry store?"

"Yep."

"Okay have fun." The manger strolled away.

I could hardly stand up when I stepped on to the large, slippery skateing rink. I clung to Seth. But that only made thing's worse. So I kinda tryed to manage on my own. "Hey, you never made it clear that we had to do something profesional on these skate's."

"Well, I have now." Rocky replyed. "Because here we are now and all we gotta do is skate a-way." He almost collided with another skater and we all laughed like crazy.

"Hey, quit that. What's so funny anyway's?"

"You are." Laughed Veronica. "Cause your the one who brought them, adn now you don't even know how to skate on them."

"Oh, yeah very funny. Neither can you."

Infact all around us there were kid's who could'nt skate. Actually what they were doing instead was either the bannana split's or the backward sommersualt. We were to. Well I was anyway's. And I thought I must be crazy to think that I would ever become a top professional ice skater. As I tryed to dance I felt the wheel's slipping away, from beneath me. Seth was keeping his cool. But I knew one fatel step would send him jiving to the floor.

Because he did'nt look at though he was trusting any step. even if he did have the aspect of perfect coolness.

'Teena-Marie's behind the groove' was ringing into our ear's and the mulitude of crazy flashing light's were dazzling into our eye's. I found myself skateing with ease at moment's. Then with panic. Then with ease again and that was miricalessy for the rest of the disco session.

After that we skated back out and it was still broad daylight. We just free-whizzed down the street, and threw our empty chip packet's and coca cola containter's into a nearby garbage bin. I was still feeling pretty dizzy. But it soon disapeared when I kept my head up into the cloud's instead of my eye's pinned to the ground.

Veronica must have enjoyed herself. Because her eye's were twinkling like I had never seen them twinkle before, although she was an Aqurious and she was laughing hysterically too.

We rounded a corner. I autmatically linked hand's with Seth and Rocky and Veronica did the same. I felt as light as a feather. Just like I could glide away into never-never land.

"Hey, you have any idea where your takeing us Rocky?" Yelled Seth.

"No. But just keep on skateing." Rocky yelled back over his shoulder. They were both ahead of us and by the way they were skateing it did'nt look as though we were headed anyway speacial.

"Im just enjoying myself." Yelled Veronica over a passing automobil.

"And look I can really skate." She held out an arm and waved it freely into the air. Then she held up her leg and she was skateing on one foot.

"Very clever." I called out. Summarly knowing that I was telling the truth and not just a blunt root-back.

It was a moment before we turned yet another corner. The sidewalk was wider. Though it still looked like a tightrope to me. Veronica unlinked her hand's from Rocky's. But Seth and I kept our's linked together for personal reason's I reckon. Not just because we knew we would both fall if we did'nt.

Veronica laughed loudly as she went along by herself. I think Rocky was about to catch up with her crazy speed because his speed suddenly shot up too. Then it was like we were all seeing a horror movie. Veronica could have stopped herself. But she did'nt. Instead her laugh's and scream's were cut short by the almost powerful impact of the autmoblil that came ploughing into her. I heard myself scream out as she was summarly hurled across the street. She lay like a tiny sparrow crumbled at the kerbside.

Rocky was screaming like crazy as he made his way stumbling across the street. "Veronica, no my baby no!"

"Rocky!" The automobil screeched into him. It had come from another direction. He was sent crashing into a streetpost.

"Rocky!" We stumbled into the street. I and Seth trying to reach Veronica the same time as Rocky.

Both car driver's had jumped out and were franticly waveing their arm's into the air. Then I saw him it was uncle Chuck. I should have known. Because his truck was the one that had ploughed mercilesly into Veronica. He ran over to her crumbled body and I followed.

"Is she okay!?" I yelled when he had gently rolled her over. He looked into my face as he took her pulse. Then slowly shook his head. "No, I'm sorry but I think she's.."

"No don't say it." I yelled. "Don't say it... please." I stared down helplessly into her open eyed face. Her brown eye's were so blank now. So desperately blank. I placed my hand over them slowly and she closed them.

Uncle Chuck had stood back up. He was mobing his brow weakly with a hankercheif.

"All I saw was this kid whizzing down toward me. Then it happened... I'm... I'm awfully sorry." I slowly took my skate's off. I ran blindly across the street. Tear's stinging my eye's to where Seth and this other guy were kneeling down beside Rocky. He was alive and he was talking now just like Daltyboy had been. In a whisper.

"Is Veronica okay?"

Seth looked up at me skeptically, as I shook my head. Rocky turned his head away in pain. "Listen.. if I don't make it... you can take the.. monney.. okay buy yourself's another treat."

"Hey, I'm so sorry I did'nt mean it." The driver dabbed franticly at Rocky's brow with a hankerchefe. "I just saw him come running out... but I tried to stop.. I did."

"It's okay." Said Seth. "Your gonna be alright.. your gonna live."

"Your stronge Rocky." I said. Tear's rolling down my face. "And your going to pull through."

Rocky smiled. Pain came across him. Tear's formed in his eye's.

"What's.. the use.. my baby's.. dead.. and..." He groaned considerbly. He gasped for breath. "And... I'm... not scared.. of..... death. I'm not afraid... of. death.."

"Rocky!" Seth yelled. "Rocky wake up!"

Rocky was motionless. I tugged at him gently. But he did'nt move. His eye's were closed. And he did'nt move. "Rocky."

The driver suddenly stopped dabbing his forehead. His face cracked. "My god... what have I done? No don't say that I killed him don't blame it all on me!" Seth took off his skate's.

We ambled slowly away from the car. Slowly away from Rocky. His badly crumbled form. Seth put out his hand to touch Veronica. She did'nt move. She was dead. I bit down hard on my lip. Uncle Chuck was still mobing his forehead weakly with his hankercheif. He pointed into the direction of a kiosk box. "It's okay he's gone to ring for an ambulance now."

As soon as he stepped out from the kiosk box I regonized him. It was the same blonde haired guy who was in the black and white photo. The one in uncle Chuck's house. He ambled back. But did'nt look at us. "It should be along now."

Seth looked at him sickly. "What good is that gonna do, both our freind's are dead and.. and.." He choked before turning away arubtly. I looked across at uncle Chuck. He gazed back at me hopelessly. He had got fatter and there were now a few wrinkle's marked clearly around his eye's.

My eye's blinked away from him wetly as the pircing sound of an ambulance came ringing from around a corner. When it screeched to a halt in front of us I could hardly bear to look as the two uniformed men carefully layed Veronica's crumpled body into a stcreacher.

They were doing the same to Rocky's along the street. Carefully putting him away into a white red crossed ambulance. Carefully putting him away for life I thought. We would never see him again. We would never see Veronica again.

They were both far away now. Both living in a different world. Where death was limited and where accident's never happened. Because this was an accident and I knew that I would never forget it as long as I was alive to remember it.

What happened after that I did'nt know. Because my mind was in a stated of greiving confusion. My heart was in painful agony every time the tragic picture flashed before my eye's. I did'nt seem to be alive anymore. I was floating into another world. I was wishing that I had been pushed away into a different corner. A peaceful corner. A corner where I would not have to grieve over the people I loved so much. A corner where there was no such thing as: death. Dying, pain, greive, good-bye's, accident's and ending happiness. But I was'nt in that corner now. I was in another corner. The real corner. And that corner had all of those thing's in it.

Like Daltyboy's death we had'nt known anything about their funeral's. All I could see was a hazy vison before me. Veronica's parent's and her sister and brother were crying as they stood before her grave. Rocky's parent's. His brother's. His sister's they were crying too. I wonderd vaugly weather they had been buried here in San Francisco. Or back home in Los Angle's. I hoped that it was here. Because I knew that I would alway's come back, to San Francisco when the sun was shining and when the bird's were singing.

The next two week's took Seth and I to my aunt's house whome I had forgot lived in San Francisco. Untill now. It was in a place called Berkeley and when my aunt opened the door she did'nt look half as surprized as I was expecting her to be. She just stared at me for a moment. Then asked us both to step on inside.

"Where have you been Livvy?" She asked slowly. When we were all sitting in her modern, blue carpeted longe. "Your mother wrote week's ago telling me that you were susposed to be comming along." I looked up into her lean, prominent fact. Took in her brown almost greying hair and her dark currious eye's which now held a few small wrinkle's underneath and finallly said: "It's been a long story."

She had listened to our story carefully like as though she had just been reading a book. Sometime's it made her wince. Sometime's it had made her smile. Now she looked at me smpathicly and said: "I'll go fix you both a nice cool drink, because you'll both be needing it, you look tuckerd." She got up, ambling away into the kitchen. I knew her house truly as though it had been my own home.

Maybe the drape's on the window had been changed. Though the room still looked the same. We had spent many happy vacation's here. My parent's, my brother and I. Not forgetting Shane my cousin who in real term's is like another brother to me. He had thought me to disco dance, and now I figured I was here to thank him for it. My aunt came back into the lounge. She was carrieing a tray. But she held something eles in her hand too. It was not untill she had sat down that I fully regonized what it was.

"Yes it's your diray Livvy. Your mother told me in her letter that she'd be expecting you to call on me sometime later and so she had it sent up to me."

I just could'nt beleive it. My heart I'm sure must have skipped a beat twice. Here after all those turmoiled week's was my beloved red dariy. As I took it from my aunt's hand I knew that the tear's were threatening to spill. Though I somehow managed to hold them back.

"My dariy – gee I'm glad it's back with me now."

"And it should be after all the days that have been missed honney." My aunt was looking at the dariy just as thoughtfully as I was. After awhile when we had finished the drink, Seth had been fully introduced she told me something about shane: "He's still in school Olivia and he's planning on going to university."

"University?" I could'nt get into my head that Shane the great king of the disco would ever want to find himself in any other role other than dancing and having a ball. He was too carefree I decieded.

"Yeah, honny and that's because he want's to become a doctor, infact honney he had dreams on becoming a top surgeon someday."

I nodded my head truly amazed.

"I've already told him that his father would have never beleived him if he had been around to even here it, though I reckon its all because he's grown out of his pastime now."

"How old is he?" I was slightly embarassed at not knowing his age so correctly. But in the whole I had quite forgotton.

"Eighteen."

"The same age as Oscar."

For the next two day's it was just like we were one happy family. I had time to be alone with my dariy again. Shower, change clothe's and wash my dandruff infested hair.

Shane was really surprized at seeing me. He had'nt changed much. Maybe his sayble hair was a little longer. But that's all. "Hey, Olivia are you still the disco queen, back home?"

We were sitting out on the lawn and the sun was shinning hotly. I looked at him smiling with the dance floor flashing my mind. "No, not anymore. though I still love it."

"Arr that's bad, cause you had the dancing abilty of a female John Travolta you know?"

"Uh huh, but you're the one who thought me after all."

"Hey, Seth what about you do you dig dancing too?" He was looking at Seth now and he smiled with that same baby smile that I've alway's admired.

"Yeah I dig it enough."

"Think you'll both be dancing when your forty?"

Seth shrugged. "That depend's on John Travolta. If he's still on the dance floor time he's a hundred. Then I guess so will we."

I laughed softly. Shane laughed too. Seth also laughed and then in no time we were all having a disscussion on long livity, disco dancing and disco music.

I had already wrote a few thing's down in my dariy. Though there was a long gap it did'nt seem to matter. I wrote down various, greivous note's on all my freind's death's. It was August 17th. I only hope that they are resting in peace. It is as though each of us are little indian's all waiting to be finally knocked off...... I am wondering who will be next....... But I am sincerly hopeing there will not be a next....

My aunt had been planning to write my mother eversince we had arrived.

But now as I ambled down the stairway I saw that she did'nt need to. Her back was turned to me and she was busy reading a letter. "Is it from mom?" I asked.

Her face looked blank when she turned around, it held no color, it almost looked as though she had been crying and her voice was weak as she answered me: "Yes Olivia... it's from your mother." Before I had time to say anything eles she had handed the letter to me and ambled out of the room. Seth came in at that moment. Again her voice sounded weak as she told him to come back out.

Full of aching currosity I unfolded the letter. The small loopy handwriting belonged umistakably to my mother. At the top left hand corner was my familular address. Further down on the right were the word's

My dear Olivia,

my baby I don't know where you are. But if you are at aunt Marth's home, which I hope you are I hope that you will come back now. Your brother and I have been searching for you every where. though now that he is resting comfortably in peace I know that he would still be hopeing his little sister's safe return. Your brother lived truly for his bike. Though now he will not be needing it anymore. Olivia if you are reading my letter I can only hope that you will understand. That you will understand what I am trying to break to you so gently because I know now you will return home. Together I am sure we will be able to get by the anguish that we sufferd over your father two year's ago.

I ask you again my baby please come home.

Your loving mother, need's you. Xxx

My heart was pounding with pain by the time I had finished reading the letter. The tear's stung my eye's like needle's. I collasped exuausted into a nearby chair. Although I understood what the word's had meant I still could'nt bring myself to beleive them. I shook my head slowly from one side to the next. Oscar. His bike. He had truly loved it. I truly loved him. Why, I thought was everything happening so fast. It had been only week's since I had left home. Only week's since I had last seen my brother. Only week's since I had last seen my mother.

Now with everything that was happening it seemed like year's. I asked myself over and over again as I numbly ambled up the stair's what I had done to deserve all this heartbreak? What had I done to deserve so many greive's in one? How I wonderd was anybody ever going to survive if there was going to be so much anguishing pain to over come before they themselve's finally died from it. Seth bumped into me as I made for my room.

"Hey, Olivïa what's matter? You look sick."

"I'm going home Seth." The word's just sprang from my mouth. He looked at me transfixed.

"Going home?"

"Yes Seth." Tear's rolled down my cheek's. "Because Oscar has just died."

"Oscar? Who's Oscar?"

He still could'nt remember who Oscar was. "My brother."

Seth numbly took the letter from my hand. His arm wrapped around me.

"Jeze I don't beleive her."

"Seth?" Our eye's met suddenly. "My... my brother has died and I'm going home I... must."

"But Livvy we had a deal we made a promise that we'd never go back again. That we'd alway's be on the road together and stay together forvever... never seperate."

"I know.. but all that's gone now... something has happened Seth..."

"Notthing's happened to part us, you don't have to go back now or ever."

"I do have to go back Seth – it's over. All my freedom life is over."

I somehow broke away from his pleading grip. He grabbed me back, swinging me around to face his pleading brown eye's. "Olivia I love you and I don't want us to end, I'm not going home ever and you don't need to go either."

I gazed at him blurrly. "Do you remember when we first met Seth... everything around us was happy then and we were both free without any greive or pain. But now everything's changed, we've changed and our plan's have to change too... I'm sorry."

Seth placed his lip's hard down on mine. "I love you Olivia."

"I love you too Seth.." I broke away from him summarly and ambled up along the hallway. He did'nt follow me. But I knew that both our heart's were aching.

My aunt and Shane had already packed to go home with me. Shane was just as greivestricken as I was. Oscar and him had been such great freind's. They had shared many thing's that as a brother and sister we had shared. Putting her case into the car. My aunt turned to gaze at me sorrowfully. "Olivia I'm glad that your going home now, your brother may have died. But your going home now to live."

I nodded my head slowly. I looked across at Seth who was standing someway off. The dariy in my hand was feeling suddenly heavy.

"Is Seth comming home too?"

"No he's told me that his life is on the road now."

"Seth." My aunt called out to him. "Your parent's will be waiting for you. Come on home now with us."

Seth said something. But did'nt come or step forward. He just stood gazing at me. I gazed back at him for a moment. My heart aching with something that I only know was greive. He looked odd now because he was wearing some of Shane's clothe's. But he still resembled the guy who I had first fell inlove with at the party. I found myself now floating back into that past. Our live's Seth's and mine. Then I suddenly found myself running over to him. "Seth you must come back home with us." We clung to each other's tightly for a moment. He gazed into my eye's and I thought he was going to come. "Olivia I love you but " He kissed me fully on the lip's. We swayed together for a moment. My aunt was calling out to me. "I can't."

"What about your parent's your brother?"

"If only we could make it together, Olivia I love you.."

"I love you too Seth." I ran blindly back to the car. My aunt and Shane were already in and climbing into a back seat I turned around waving at the lonesome, familular figure who I had alway's loved and still did. The car pulled away. My thought's were everywhere. But now I knew I was going home. Going home to my mother.

When the car pulled to a stop outside the familiar house. My heart ached considerbly with greive. It was there that the pass came floating back to me again. My mother, Oscar and I were just moveing into our new house. We were moveing into 2755 Lemond street, on the westside of the avenue and we were all getting ready to start a new life after my father's death. Now it was as though history was reapeating it'self. I slowly got out of the car and I gazed at my old familular street. My familular house. I was at that very moment surrounded in the past, and the disco light's were flashing in my mind. School and Season.

The front door opened and my mother and I collasped into each other's outstreached arm's. "My baby.. Olivia I knew you'd come back home."

"I'm home now mom." I gasped. "Home to stay." She had changed so much. Her hair had gone grey and brittle. She was frail, almost lifeless and the skin around her eye's had screacthed so much that a few wrinkle's were shown. Her dark eye's searched mine now. They were filled with greive, with pain and I knew that mine held the same. "Olivia he died so bitterly. But I know that your brother rest's in peace now."

I nodded my head. The tear's of greive brimming over with painful hottness. "It's all my fault... I'm sorry too moma.. and he'll alway's rest in peace.. I know."

"Don't blame it on yourself my baby... my other baby died because the lord is his father... and he know's how to take care of his children even if they do die on the road and on moterbike's."

The four of us sat inside of my familular purple carpeted lounge. The lounge were my mother, Oscar and I had sat cozily watching t.v. or playing backgammon, together. We wer'nt doing those now. But we were sitting quitely in greive. Remembering the good time's of somebody who was now resting safely in the hand's of god. "How did it happen?" I managed to say after awhile.

My mother gazed at me sorrowfully. "Your brother loved that bike, and he loved roaming around on it too they were comming into Los Angle's some other kid's on bike's and Oscar happened to be heading in their direction and so my baby died in that bikewreck, it had been all over in a moment."

"Did did he die instanstly?" I asked and my mind was travelling back to the time when comming out from a disco one night we had been chased by a gang of motorbiked youth's. I wonderd vaugly weather they could have been the same.

"Yes... Livvy he died instantly. They took him into hospital. But he was dead on arrival."

"Was it.. last... last night?"

"Lastnight Olivia at 11.30... and I know the lord did'nt let him suffer any pain, he was a good boy, a good brother to you and now he's alright. Resting in the arm's of his father."

I lowerd my head and my heart ached. Resting in the arm's of his father. In the arm's of our father. He is a good boy, a good brother and because he loved his bike to much his father has taken him into his arm's and given him a love that is far greater than the love that he gave for his bike.

At the funeral it was raining. Though I knew that the rain could not disrubt a funeral that was already to greivingly overpowerd. We stood over the gave. My aunt's, my uncle's, my mother, Shane and I. The ceremony was breif though when it was over the tear's in our eye's and the drop's of pouring rain mixed in one. There were time's when I thought the tear's would never stop. But I knew that the ache in my heart would never leave. It would be there all the time. Stored away someplace at the bottom of my heart where it would someday finally take it over and truly break it to notthingness.

September 22nd

August 19th was the day my mother and I finally left westside avenue for life. We could'nt like we could'nt bear the pain of reliving my father's memorie's, bear the pain of reliving Oscar's memorie's. So we had it settled that all of us would live together in my aunt's house. Before we left behind the tragic past I found myself walking lonesomely up the avenue. I walked around all the west.

Takeing in all the familuar house's, sidewalk's, tree's and store's. I gazed out toward my high school remembering clearly some of the goodtime's. I amble up my freind's street's knowing that all along even if they we'ret there that their parent's and brother's or sister's were still there. I ambled up Seth's street and I gazed at the shaddowy willowed tree that stood swaying fornelly beside his house, outside his bedroom window.

When I knocked at his front door my schoolbook's were with me. He would open the door and together we would catch a ride to school on the southside bus. The door did open. But Seth's brown eye's wer'nt gazing at me. Instead they were the eye's of his mother and they looked knowinlg pained. But currious. "Yes, what is it?" She asked. "Have you brought my boy back home?"

I suddenly found it hard to talk. The lump in my throat increased. though I finally managed. "I.. I've just come to tell..."

"Don't tell me anything that I already know... if Seth dos'nt want to come on home then he has his own mind."

"He.. he's still on the road... I tried talking him to come back. But he won't."

"No need telling me what he's like, because I already know When he's ready. he's ready." She ambled away from the doorway summeraly. I was looking into his eye's the next moment. He looked so much like his brother. His dark hair was the same and so was his lean, handsome face. But he was about a foot taller, and he was'nt smiling just stareing.

"Hey, that's great your back but he is'nt." His voice even sounded like Seth's. It gave me the feeling that I was truly seeing Seth.

"Are you sorry your brother ran off like that?"

"I don't care. He's a dumbhunk anyway's running away like as though he has'nt got a decent home to live in and a bed to sleep in... he'll come home when he want's."

"I just hope he come's home soon."

"Yeah well you can keep serching for him even if it's at the end of the world. But I know he'll be the one to decide when he's found cause he's my brother and

I know him like I know my ownself." He suddenly ambled away and came back again carrieing something. "Here take this, it'll rimind you of what he look's like."

He handed me a photograph of Seth. I regonized it as one of his school photo's because he was wearing that old blue sweatshirt of his. I handed it back after a moment. "I'll alway's remember Seth, what he look's like so I won't be needing it."

He handed it back to me. "Go on take it, cause every girl has a picture of their boyfreind to place on their bedroom dresser's."

I took it again trying hard to swallow the large lump in my trought and at the same time trying to smile. "Okay, thankyou.."

"Jessie."

"Jessie thank's I'll take it... so long."

"Goodbye – Olivia."

I ambled slowly back onto the sidewalk. He had closed the door before I even had the chance to look back. Just to see Seth again I guess. Standing as he was in his faded blue jean's and bleached blue tee-shirt. I continued to walk along the street's after that. Every street corner where Seth had kissed me and I him gazed down at his photo and experinced that same feeling.

I ambled into some of the park's that we had been in, and touched the grass knowing that it would truly never change. I ambled along to the disco club. It was closed down now, with the window's boarded up and numerous of scrawled painted letter's showerd along the wall's. It was here that I felt America's youth had disapeared. Not a single teen-ager was in sight. Everything around me was so lonesome, quite and empty. I thought of all the day's when the street would be full of disco goer's. Teen-ager's of every size, color and height would be swarming along the sidewalk, heading directly for the disco door's. I continued to amble on down the empty, silent street. The sky looked dark and I knew it was about to rain. There I stood for awhile in my pale summer dress, my slickbacked sandle's and the photo of Seth held in my hand. I gazed around at the street of my youth. I rememberd the day's of the disco revoloution. The day's when discomania was at it's toll. Then truly I knew that none but one had managed to survive.

ENDING ONE

The truck rumbled past me. A faint sound of music caught my ear's. For some strange reson I stopped walking. The rumbling stopped as the truck skidded, pulling up somway behind me. A door slammed. Dust swirled the air. The truck rumbled on. Another figure was standing in the street. As it ambed slowly toward me the music cresendoed. I regonized the walk. Shane's old clothe's. The darkbrown hair, sensual brown eye's. Oh my god. A name sprang from my mouth: "Seth!" And it began to rain. "Olivia!"

"Your back – Seth you've come back!"

"Olivia I love you!"

I found myself walking. Walking toward him. Tear's sprang from my eye's.

The music had stopped. Seth no longer held the radio. Our shaddow's were touching. The sun peeked out from behind a dark cloud. As I held out my arm's. As he held out his arm's. His picture slipped from my hand, and I suddenly knew that as we gazed into each other's eye's this would alway's be far more greater than any.... discomania..........

ENDING TWO

I am sixteen now. The music blared out. The red light's flashed with vigor.

Standing in the crowded disco I slowly began to dance. The record was one of Michale Jackson's, 'I want to rock with you.' takeing a sip of my orange soda pop I was lost to the world.

"Hey, how does it feel to be sixteen?"

The word's were so familular. I summarly turned around. The eroctic, sensual, brown eye's of somebody I onced loved. Still loved were gazing into me. "Terrific." I said.

"Dynamic."

"And how does it feel to be sixteen for you?"

Seth threw up his arm's in to the hot air. "Beautiful sexy, something like you."

Seth came back, and before I had enough time to jot it down in my beloved red dairy we were going out with each other something that I thought would alway's be far greater than any... discomania........

SOME POST-DISCOITAL WORDS FROM THE EDITORS:

After we very happily became close friends with the fabulous June-Alison Gibbons, June-Alison generously gave us her extensive archive of writings and artworks by her and her twin-sister, Jennifer. We three would often discuss the many lovely projects that we would undertake with the many shining treasures in this gorgeous collection that we named "The Magickal Twins Collection".

One fine day we were — sadly! — lamenting to June-Alison about the sad loss of Jennifer's novel *Discomania*, which we believed, like all other enthusiasts of her and her sister's astonishing works, to be — sadly! — lost. June-Alison answered cryptically — but since she often responds to us cryptically, her new crypticism didn't surprise us too much — although, although... such a response normally means something cool is arising.

Then, some few days later, during a phone call to arrange one of her sweet visits to stay with us in Hastings, June-Alison suddenly, shockingly, told us that she still had Jennifer's typescript for *Discomania*.

Whilst June-Alison was typing up her *The Pepsi-Cola Addict* in their bedroom, Jennifer was typing up *Discomania* on the same desk beside her. Both of them submitted their books to the English vanity press New Horizon. *The Pepsi-Cola Addict* was accepted. But New Horizon rejected *Discomania* for being "too violent, too sexual, and too futuristic" — it's almost unheard of for a vanity press to reject a book, unless there are clear legal reasons to do so — and Jennifer was heart-broken. After the typescript was returned to Jennifer, June-Alison kept hold of it, knowing that one day a publisher would appear to her and Jennifer. And here we — Cashen's Gap and Strange Attractor — came, and appeared!

Holograph pages in our The Magickal Twins Collection show that June-Alison offered suggestions to Jennifer for *Discomania*, and that Jennifer also made comments on June-Alison's *The Pepsi-Cola Addict*. On the endpapers of the hardback edition of this novel, one can see four sides of Jennifer's handwritten notes for this novel. On the paperback's endpapers we have reproduced pages from Jennifer's typescript for *Discomania*.

Jennifer wrote two different, single-page, endings for *Discomania*. Both of them are added as the final two pages of the book, and clearly marked.

So here at last is the violent, sexual, futuristic classic — hot, burnin', groovin', killin', shakin', funkin', sexy, sexin', utterly beyond — for the first time ever — *Discomania*!

Dearest Jennifer, Dearest June-Alison — we, and all your fans, are OverMoon that your Disco Is At Last Open. It's an Inferno!

Ania Goszczyńska and David Tibet, Hastings, St. Valentine's Day For Us All, 2025.

ACKNOWLEDGEMENTS

Ania, David, Jamie, and Mark would like to thank Jennifer and June-Alison for their kind permission to publish *Discomania*. The typescript and holograph pages of *Discomania*, and the photographs of Jennifer Gibbons, are in The PolkAnok Collection of Ania Goszczyńska and David Tibet, courtesy of the generosity of June-Alison and Jennifer Gibbons.

Ania, David, Jennifer, and June-Alison would like to thank Bea Turner for her beautiful work in transcribing Jennifer's complex and exquisitely unpredictable typescript — a very remarkable feat!

Ania, David, Jamie, Mark, Jennifer, and June-Alison also thank greatly Richard Bancroft for his proofing and Hiba Shahtoot for applying them.

Our thanks to Fraser Carr Miles of Bracken Books for scanning the holographs and typescript, and to Ossian Brown and Julian Kalinowski for their great help on this project.

Ania and David would like to thanks Jamie, Mark, and Strange Attractor deeply for their support and friendship — it's a delight to work with you. This book is a collaboration between Strange Attractor and Cashen's Gap.

STRANGE ATTRACTOR PRESS
CASHEN'S GAP
2026